THE ULTIMATE
SANTA-BANTA JOKE BOOK

THE ULTIMATE
SANTA-BANTA JOKE BOOK

RUPA

First published by
Rupa Publications India Pvt. Ltd 2014
7/16, Ansari Road, Daryaganj
New Delhi 110002

Sales Centres:

Allahabad Bengaluru Chennai
Hyderabad Jaipur Kathmandu
Kolkata Mumbai

ISBN: 978-81-291-3257-4

Second impression 2014

10 9 8 7 6 5 4 3 2

The moral right of the author has been asserted.

Printed at Thomson Press India Ltd, Faridabad

Not at Home!

A visitor to Santa: Which one is Mr Banta's flat?

Santa: Please come with me.

The visitor is taken to the third floor.

The visitor rings the bell and there is no response. He repeatedly rings the doorbell and still no one answers.

Visitor: I think he is not in.

Santa: Yeah, he has gone out. He'll be back in the evening.

Bank Robbers!

Santa and Banta decided to rob a bank but mess it up during the robbery. However, they do manage to escape with two sacks and divide it amongst themselves

When they meet again, they ask each other what did they find in the sack.

Banta: Ten lakh rupees!

Santa: Wow... that's a lot of money. What did you do with the cash?

Banta: I bought a house. How about your sack?

Santa: It was full of bills.

Banta: And what did you do with them?

Santa: Eh, well... I am paying them off little by little.

Company Policy!

An eager Banta, entered his prospective boss's office for an interview.

'One thing our company is very particular about is cleanliness. I hope you wiped your shoe on the door mat while coming in?' asked the boss.

'Yes sir,' Banta replied promptly.

The boss continued, 'Another thing we're very particular about is honesty. There is no door mat outside!'

Fussy Wife

Banta had been arrested and was presented before the judge.

The judge asked, 'Do you admit you broke into the same clothes shop three times?'

'Yes,' replied Banta.

'Could you please tell the court what you stole?' asked the judge.

'I stole a dress, your honour,' Banta said.

'Just one dress? But you admitted to breaking in three times,' the judge remarked.

'Yes I did, your honour,' said Banta. 'But on two of those occasions, I broke in to return the dress I took before.'

'Return the dress? Why? I don't understand,' said the judge.

'Because my wife, Preeto, didn't like the design, your honour.'

Second appendix!

Santa called the doctor at 2.00 a.m. 'Doc, my wife is having severe abdomen pain. I think it's her appendix.'

'What nonsense!' said the doctor sleepily. 'I took out your wife's appendix two years ago. Go back to sleep.'

Five minutes later, the phone rings and it's Santa again.

'Doc, I'm sure it's her appendix.'

'Oh God!' the doctor groaned. 'Did you ever hear of anyone having a second appendix?'

'No,' said Santa. 'But I'm sure you must have heard of someone having a second wife!'

The Gorilla Catcher!

A man woke up one morning and found a gorilla on his roof. He looked up the yellow pages and sure enough, there was an advertisement for 'Gorilla Catchers'. He called the number and the gorilla catcher, Santa, said he would be over in thirty minutes.

Thirty minutes later, Santa reached the spot with a ladder, a baseball, a shotgun and a huge dog.

'What are you going to do,' asked the house owner.

Santa said, 'I'm going to climb up the ladder to reach the roof and knock the gorilla off with this baseball bat. When the gorilla falls to the ground, the dog will grab it's testicles and squeeze. The gorilla will then be subdued in order for me to put him in the cage in the back of the van.'

He hands the shotgun to the house owner.

'What's the shotgun for?' asked the house owner.

Santa replied, 'If the gorilla knocks me off the roof, shoot the dog.'

Classic Insult!

Santa and a girl were standing at the bus stop.
Santa to the girl: Nice lipstick.
Girl: Thanks.
Santa: Nice clothes
Girl: Thanks.
Santa: Nice earrings
Girl: Thanks.
Santa: Nice necklace.
Girl: Thank you so much, bhaiya.
Santa: Very strange, phir bhi tum sundar nahi lag rahi ho.

Happy Married Life

Banta asked Santa, 'What is the secret behind your happy married life?'

Santa said, 'You should share responsibilities with due love and respect for each other. Then there will be no problems.'

Banta asked, 'Can you explain?'

Santa replied, 'In my house, I take the big decisions whereas my wife decides on smaller issues. We do not interfere in each others' decisions.'

Still not convinced, Banta asked him to give him some examples.

Santa said, 'Smaller issues like which car should we buy, how much money do we need to save, when to visit our home town, which sofa, air-conditioner, refrigerator to buy, how to manage the monthly expenses, whether to keep a maid are decided by my wife. I just agree to it.'

Banta asked, 'Then what is your role?'

Santa said, 'My decisions are only for very big issues. Like whether America should attack Syria, whether the European Union should lift sanctions over Zimbabwe, whether Tendulkar should retire, Salman Khan's Marriage etc.'

Mouse Trap

Santa: I'm in big trouble!

Banta: Why is that?

Santa: I saw a mouse in my house!

Banta: Oh, well, all you need to do is use a trap.

Santa: I don't have one.

Banta: Well then, buy one.

Santa: Can't afford one.

Banta: I can give you mine if you want.

Santa: That sounds good.

Banta: All you need to do is just use some cheese in order to make the mouse come to the trap.

Santa: I don't have any cheese.

Banta: Okay then, take a piece of bread and put a bit of oil on it and put it in the trap.

Santa: I don't have oil.

Banta: Well, then put only a small piece of bread.

Santa I don't have bread.

Banta: Then what the hell is that mouse doing in your house???

Money Well Spent

Santa walked into a bar and asked the bartender, 'Was I in here last night?'

'You certainly were,' replied the bartender.

'And did I spend a lot of money?' Santa asked.

'You spent over ₹10,000,' the bartender said.

'Thank God for that,' said Santa. 'I thought I'd wasted it.'

World Record Skydiving Stunt

Santa and Banta, two sky divers having tried all the ordinary stunts, decided to set a world record by free falling to within 100 feet of the ground, before opening their chutes.

Having jumped from 8000 feet, the two came plummeting towards the earth.

When his altimeter read 100, Banta shouted to Santa, 'Now?'

'No, not now!'

'Now?' Banta screamed at 50 feet.

'Not yet!'

'Come on,' Banta shrieked, 'it's only 10 feet!'

'For God's sake, Banta,' Santa yelled, 'haven't you ever fallen from ten feet before?'

Parrot Action

Santa went to an auction and bid for a parrot. He bid 1000 rupees, but someone else quoted 2000.

Santa bid 2500 rupees, but someone else bid 3000 Rupees.

Santa bid 3500 rupees, but someone else bid 4000 Rupees.

Santa was determined to buy the bird and put in a final bid of 4500 Rupees. This time there were no other bids and the parrot was sold to Santa.

'That's a lot of money I've paid for this bird,' said Santa to the auctioneer. 'I hope he can talk.'

'Of course he can,' replied the auctioneer. 'Who do you think was bidding against you?'

Swollen Foot

Santa goes to the podiatrist with a swollen foot. After a careful examination, the doctor hands him a pill that looks big enough to choke a horse.

'I will be right back with some water,' the doctor tells him.

The doctor has been gone a while, and Santa is losing his patience. He hobbles outside to the drinking fountain, forces the pill down his throat and gobbles down water until the pill has been swallowed.

He then hobbles back into the examining room. Just then the doctor comes back with a bucket of warm water.

'Ok, after the tablet dissolves, soak that foot for about twenty minutes.'

Stuttering Problem!

Banta, although ordinarily eloquent, had a problem of stuttering when excited.

Once, when walking with his friend, Santa, down a crowded city street, he said with great excitement, 'L-l-l-l-look at that g-g-g-girl. W-w-w-what a f-f-f-f-f-figure!'

'Where? Where?' asked Santa, equally excited.

'Too late,' said Banta, quite calm. 'She walked into a building.'

A moment later, he said, 'L-l-l-l-look at that c-c-c-car. N-n-n-n- never saw s-s-s-s-s----'

'Where? Where?' demanded Santa again.

'Turned the corner,' said Banta briefly.

A few minutes passed and Banta said again, 'L-l-l-l-l-look...'

Santa, weary of having everything over before Banta could finish, said, 'It's all right. I see, I see...'

There was a brief pause and then Banta said, 'If you saw it, why did you step on it?'

Slipping Lion!

Santa came back from a safari in Africa. Upon arrival, he went to his friend Banta, and told him about his adventures.

'I was out in the jungle,' he said, 'when all of a sudden I heard a noise in the bush behind me. Looking back, I saw a huge lion, licking his chops and smiling at me. The lion started coming my way and I started running, with the lion not far behind. When the lion was almost at my neck, he suddenly slipped and I got ahead a bit.

'The lion started gaining on me and as he got closer, once again he slipped. I happened to see a house not far away and dashed towards it.

As I got close to the house, the lion was almost on top of me, when he slipped for a third time. With the very last bit of strength, I ran into the house and closed the door in the lion's face.'

'Wow! That's some story,' said Banta. 'If I'd been in that situation, I would have shit my pants.'

'Well, what do you think the lion kept slipping on?'

The Last Hope!

Santa had just finished collecting the rent from the tenants in his apartment block. But when he got home he realized that his wallet was missing and he burst into tears.

'What's the matter?' asked his wife.

'I've lost my wallet containing twenty-five thousand rupees,' he wailed. 'I think I put it in the inside pocket of my coat, but it's not there now.'

'Did you look in your pant pockets?'

'Yes, but the money isn't there either.'

'What about the side pocket of your jacket? Did you look there?'

'Of course not!' he snapped. 'Do you want me to lose the last bit of hope I have?'

Whose Problem is it Really?

Banta feared his wife Preeto wasn't hearing as well as she used to and might need a hearing aid. Not quite sure how to approach her, he called the family doctor to discuss the problem.

The doctor told him about a simple informal test he could perform to give him a better idea about her hearing loss.

'Here's what you do,' said the Doctor. 'Stand about 40 feet away from her and speak in a normal conversational tone to see if she hears you. If not, stand 30 feet away, then 20 feet, and so on until you get a response.'

That evening, Preeto was in the kitchen cooking dinner and Banta was in the living room. He thought to himself, 'I'm about 40 feet away, let us' see what happens.'

Then in a normal tone he asks, 'Preeto ji, what's for dinner?'

No response.

Banta moves closer to the kitchen, about 30 feet from Preeto and repeats, 'Preeto ji, what's for dinner?'

Still no response.

Next he moves into the dining room where he is about 20 feet from her and asks, 'Preeto ji, what's for dinner?'

Again he gets no response.

So, he walks up to the kitchen door, about 10 feet away and asks, 'Preeto ji, what's for dinner?'

Again there is no response.

So he walks right up behind her, 'Preeto ji, what's for dinner?'

For God's sake, Banta ji, for the FIFTH time, 'BIRYANI!'

Horse Keeping

Banta wanted to board his horse. The first farmer he asked said he would keep it at ₹250 a day, plus he would keep the manure.

Banta thought that was too high and went to another farmer. His price was ₹200 per day plus he would get to keep the manure.

Then he went to Santa who asked for just ₹50 a day.

Banta asked, 'Don't you want to keep the manure?'

Santa said, 'At ₹50 a day, there won't be any!'

Diamond Ring

In the midst of a hectic day at office, Santa got a phone call from his friend Banta.

Banta: Santa, I just bought an expensive diamond ring for my wife, Preeto. I hope this won't break up our long friendship?

Santa: Hey Banta! Have you gone crazy? Why should your buying your wife an expensive diamond ring break up our friendship? After all, you are not taking it to my wife.

Banta: But my wife is taking it to your wife. She is over to your house right now, showing it to your wife.

Unbeatable Logic!

Santa decided to study for the MBA exam. He was able to understand everything except the logic part. One day when he was studying, one of his friends came home.

Friend: Santa, how is your MBA preparation?

Santa: Everything is fine, but I cannot understand logic.

Friend: Logic is very easy.

Santa: Can you give me an example so that I can understand?

Friend: Okay. Do you have fish pot in your house?

Santa: Yes.

Friend: Logically, there will be water in it.

Santa: Yes.

Friend: Logically, there will be fish in it.

Santa: Yes.

Friend: Logically, someone will be feeding the fish.

Santa: Yes.

Friend: I take a guess that your wife will be feeding the fish.

Santa: Yes.

Friend: so, logically, your are married.

Santa: Yes.

Friend: So, that means you are a heterosexual.

Santa was very glad at having understood the concept of logic. Next day he sees Banta who was also preparing for MBA exams.

Santa: How is your MBA preparation?

Banta: Everything is fine except for logic.

Santa: Oh, logic is easy.

Banta: Please, give me an example.

Santa: Do you have a fish pot in your house?

Banta: No, I don't.

Santa: Oh my God! That means you're gay!

Santa on KBC!

Santa couldn't believe the fact thathe'd made it to the last round of his favourite game show, *Kaun Banega Crorepati*.

'Congratulations, Santa ji,' said Big B. 'Answer correctly and you go home with five crore!'

'This is a two-part question on Punjab history,' he continued. 'The second half of the question is always easier. Which part would you like first?'

Santa figured he'd play it safe. 'I think I'll try the second part of the question first.'

Big B nodded approvingly, while the audience was silent with anticipation.

'Okay, Santa ji, here is your question: and in which year did it happen?'

Take the Soup

Santa was in the hospital for a complete check-up. At 11.00 a.m., they brought him soup for lunch which he refused.

At 2.00 p.m., they again tried to serve him some soup, which he refused yet again.

They tried again at 5.00 p.m. and 7.00 p.m. and both times Santa turned down the soup. Finally, they gave up.

In preparation for the next day's test, they entered his room at 3.00 a.m., 4.00 a.m, and 6.00 a.m. to give him an enema.

When Santa got home from the hospital after the tests, he told his wife, Jeeto, 'Whatever you do, if you go to that hospital and they try to serve you soup, take it! If you refuse it, they sneak in while you're asleep and shove it up your ass.'

Neighbour's Wife

Banta had been admiring his neighbour's wife who always greeted him with a seductive smile. Banta didn't know how to approach her to tell her of his desire as she was married. However, one day the lady herself approached Banta when he was alone in his apartment.

Banta: Hi.

Lady: Hi.

Banta: Is everything alright?

Lady: Yes. Just need little help from you (Smiling seductively).

Banta: Wow! Anything for the angel.

Lady: I...I...I...just don't know how to say this. I'll be so ashamed of myself if I ask and you say no.

Banta: Oh my lady, you don't have to. I am ready to do anything for you.

Lady: You know, it's been over three weeks since my husband is travelling.

Banta: Yes! Yes! Yes!

Lady: And even when he's around, he has some...he has some disabilities.

Banta: Oh poor you. You must have been going through hell!

Lady: I know you'll be stronger than him.

Banta: Sure.

Lady: Can you help me?

Banta: Wow! Now? Sure, I'm ready if you are ready.

Lady: Oh thank goodness! That's why I came to you. Can you help me carry our deep freezer from the kitchen to the next street for repairs?

The Definition of Slow!

Santa was a slow worker and found it difficult to hold down a job. After a visit to the job center he was offered work at the local zoo.

When he arrived at work on his first day, the keeper, aware of Santa's reputation, told him to take care of the tortoise section.

Later, the keeper dropped by to see how Santa was getting on and found him standing by an empty enclosure.

'Where are the tortoises?' he asked him.

'I can't believe it,' said Santa. 'I just opened the door and then.....Whooooosh!'

Blind Date!

Santa sets up Banta for a blind date with one of his friends. But Banta is a little worried about going out with someone he has never seen before.

'What do I do if she's ugly?' says Banta. 'I'll be stuck with her all night.'

'Don't worry.' Santa says. 'Just go up to her door and meet her first. If you like what you see, then everything goes as planned. If you don't, just shout "Aaauuuggghhh" and fake an asthma attack.'

So that night, Banta knocks at Shirley's door. When she comes out he is awe-struck by her beauty and sexiness. Banta's about to speak when the girl suddenly shouts, 'Aaauuuggghhh!'

What a Relief!

Banta tripped on the stairs and broke his leg. The doctor put a cast on it and warned that he wasn't to use the stairs until the cast came off.

Weeks later, the doctor removed the cast and pronounced him well on the way to recovery.

'Oh good,' Banta said. 'Is it all right for me to take the stairs now?'

'Yes,' said the doctor, 'if you promise to be careful.'

'I can't tell you what a relief it will be,' he sighed. 'It was such a nuisance crawling outside and shinnying up and down that drainpipe all the time!'

Weird Dreams!

Preeto went to see a psychiatrist to discuss her husband Santa.

'Doctor, my husband has this problem. Almost every night he dreams he's a refrigerator!'

'My dear, that is not really a problem! A lot of people dream that they are somebody or something unusual.'

Preeto leans forward and softly whispers. 'But you see doctor it is also a problem for me! Santa sleeps with his mouth open and his little light keeps me awake!'

Remedy for Hiccups!

Santa went into a drug store and asked the pharmacist if he could give him something for hiccups.

Without warning, the pharmacist leaned ahead and slapped Santa hard across the face.

'What did you do that for?' asked Santa indignantly.

'Well, you haven't got hiccups any more, have you?'

'I haven't got hiccups; my wife has!' replied Santa!

New Chauffeur!

Santa hired a new chauffeur.

Jeeto asked the chauffer to take her out for shopping and was very shaken by the experience.

Back home, she pleaded with Santa, 'Please dear, you must sack this new chauffeur at once. He is so rash he nearly killed me three times this morning.'

'Darling, don't be so hasty,' replied Santa, 'give him another chance.'

Suppositories for Constipation!

A doctor prescribed suppositories to Santa, who was suffering from constipation. A week later, he returned to the doctor and complained that the treatment wasn't working.

'Have you been taking them regularly?' asked the doctor.

'What do you think I've been doing?' snapped Santa. 'Shoving them up my ass?'

The Weekend Party!

One Friday, Santa left work early, but instead of going home, he spent the weekend partying with the boys. When he finally returned home on Sunday night, his wife, Jeeto, got on his case.

After a few of hours of swearing and screaming, his wife paused and pointed at him and made him an offer, 'How would you like it if you didn't see me for a couple of days?'

The husband couldn't believe his luck, so he looked up, smiled and said, 'That would suit me just fine!!'

Monday went by and he didn't see his wife. Tuesday and Wednesday went by and he still didn't see her.

Came Thursday, the swelling went down a bit and he could see her a little out of the corner of his left eye.

Anniversary Gift!

Santa was in trouble as he had forgotten his wedding anniversary. Jeeto, his wife, was really pissed.

She told him, 'Tomorrow morning, I expect to find a gift in the driveway that goes from 0 to two hundred in 10-15 seconds AND IT BETTER BE THERE!'

The next morning Santa got up early and left for work. When Jeeto woke up, she looked out of the window and sure enough there was a gift-wrapped box in the middle of the driveway.

Confused, Jeeto put on her robe and ran out to the driveway and brought the box back in the house.

She opened it and found a brand new bathroom scale.

Santa has been missing since Friday.

Bathing Santa!

Banta came to meet Santa at his house.

He knocked at the door and was surprised to see a stark naked Santa dripping with water.

'Come on Santa, aren't you ashamed? Why don't you wear something?', said Banta.

Santa, sheepishly ran into the bathroom and came back wearing his slippers.

Thankful Santa!

Santa shook his doctor's hand in gratitude and said, 'Since we are the best of friends, I would not want to insult you by offering payment. But I would like for you to know that I have mentioned you in my will'.

'That is very kind of you,' said the doctor emotionally and then added, 'Can I see that prescription I just gave you? I'd like to make a little change.'

Deep Trouble

Santa and Banta decide to apply for jobs at a mine that had opened nearby. After sitting in the waiting room for a while, Banta gets called in for his interview.

The boss asks Banta if he had worked in underground mines before. Banta says that he had.

The boss asks him how deep under the ground had he worked.

Banta says, 'Oh, about 8 to 10 feet.'

The boss says, 'Mines are a lot deeper than that. Get out of here you're no miner!'

On his way out, Banta tells Santa to tell the boss that he

worked real deep under the ground so he could get the job. Santa gets called in.

The boss asks Santa if he had worked in underground mines before.

Santa says, 'Oh sure.'

The boss asks how deep under the ground had he worked.

Santa says, 'I used to work in a mine that was 20,000 feet under the ground.'

The boss says, '20,000 feet, Wow! That is incredible! What kind of lights did you use for a mine so deep?'

Santa says, 'Oh, I didn't need a light. I worked the day shift!'

Vegetarian Chicken

Each Friday night after work, Santa would fire up his outdoor grill and cook a tandoori chicken and some meat kebabs. Since all his neighbours were strict Catholics and it was the period of Lent, they were forbidden from eating chicken and meat on Fridays.

The delicious aroma from the grilled meats was causing such a problem that the neighbours finally talked to their Priest. The Priest came to visit Santa and suggested that he become a Catholic.

After several classes and much study, Santa attended Mass and as the priest sprinkled holy water over him, he said, 'You were born a Sikh, and raised a Sikh, but now, you are a Catholic.'

Santa's neighbours were greatly relieved until Friday night arrived. The wonderful aroma of tandoori chicken and meat kebabs filled the neighbourhood.

The Priest was called immediately by the neighbours and as he rushed into Santa's backyard, clutching a rosary and ready to scold him, he stopped and watched in amazement.

There stood Santa, holding a small bottle of holy water which he carefully sprinkled over the grilling meats and chanted: 'Oye, you were born a chicken, and you were born a lamb, you were raised a chicken, and you were raised a lamb but now yara, you are potato and tomato'!

Wet Dreams

Banta complained to a doctor that he wet his bed every night.

'Do you get any dreams before that happens?' the doctor asked.

'Yes, doctor. Usually, I see a dream in which a small demon comes and says, 'Let's pee.''

'OK,' the doctor said. 'Next time you see the demon, say, 'No, we've already peed.''

On his next visit, the doctor asked Banta, 'So, did you do as I said?'

'Yes, I did.'

'Did it help?'

'No, doctor. It only made the matter worse.'

'How?'

'As I said "We've already peed," the demon nodded and said, "Then, let's shit a little."'

My Wife is Expecting

'How does Jeeto like being pregnant?' Santa asked his friend, Banta.

'Oh, she's not pregnant,' Banta replied, 'she's expecting.'

'What's the difference?' Santa pressed.

'Well,' Banta explained, 'She's expecting me to cook dinner, she's expecting me to do the housework, she's expecting me to rub her feet...'

Constipated Horse

Banta owned a big farm. He had lots of animals like pigs, chickens, horses and cows.

One day, one of his horses became constipated. Banta went to the vet who gave him some big pills and a pipe. The doctor instructed him to put a pill in the pipe, stick the pipe up the horse's ass and blow as hard as he could.

Banta went home and did exactly what the vet told him to do.

An hour later, Banta came back to the doctor's place looking very sick. The doctor asked what was wrong.

Then Banta replied, 'The horse blew first.'

Men Are Better Friends Than Women

One night Jeeto doesn't return home.

The next morning when Banta demands to know where she was all night, she claims she stayed at a friend's house.

Banta rings up ten of her best friends and they all say Jeeto didn't stay at their place last night.

One night Banta doesn't return home.

The next morning when Jeeto demands to know where he was all night, he claims he stayed at a friend's house.

Jeeto rings up ten of his best friends. Eight of them say Banta did stay at their place last night and the other two claim he is still there!

Visiting a Friend

Banta goes over to visit one of his friends.

While he is at his friend's place, it starts raining very heavily.

His friend tells him to spend the night at his house and go home the next day.

When he hears this, Banta rushes out of the door and comes a while later totally drenched and carrying a small bag.

His friend asks, 'Where did you run off too!'

Bant says, 'I went home to get my pyjamas!'

Santa's Logic?

Cop: How did you kill fifty people in a car crash?

Santa: I suddenly lost control.

Cop: Then what happened?

Santa: I saw two people on the right and a wedding party on the left. You tell me which should I have hit?

Cop: The two people on the right would have certainly caused less damage.

Santa: Exactly what I thought! I hit the first one but then the other one person ran into the wedding so I went after him!

Gotcha!

Farmer Banta, killed a lamb and hung it up for the night, intending to butcher it in the morning, but the next day it was gone.

He didn't tell a soul about it and nothing happened for

more than two months.

Then another farmer, Santa, who lived down the road, came by and said, 'By the way Banta, did you ever find out who stole your lamb?'

'Nope,' said Banta. 'Not until just now.'

Stung by a Bee

Stung by a bee, Santa comes running to the doctor shouting and screaming in pain

Sana: Please doctor you've got to help me. I've been stung by a bee.

Doctor: Don't worry; I'll put some cream on it.

Santa: You will never find that bee. It must be miles away by now.

Doctor: No you don't understand! I'll put some cream on the place you were stung.

Santa: Oh! It happened in the garden where I was sitting under a tree.

Doctor (in anger): No, no you IDIOT! I mean, on which part of your body did that bee sting?

Santa (still screaming in pain): On my finger! The bee stung me on my finger and it really hurts.

Doctor (banging his fist, abusing and shouting): Which one?

Santa (innocently): How am I to know? All bees look the same to me.

Smart Answer

Santa and his wife, Jeeto were sitting around the breakfast table one lazy Sunday morning.

Santa said to her, 'If I were to die suddenly, I want you to immediately sell all my stuff.'

'Now why would you want me to do something like that?' she asked.

'I figure that you would eventually remarry and I don't want some other jerk using my stuff.'

Jeeto looked at Santa and said, 'What makes you think I'd marry another jerk?'

Next Baby

Santa picked up his wife Jeeto and their new baby from the hospital and brought them home.

It was not long before Jeeto suggested that Santa try his hand at changing a diaper.

'I'm busy,' he said. 'I promise I'll do the next one.'

The next time soon came around, so Jeeto asked him again.

Santa looked at Jeeto and said innocently, 'I didn't mean the next diaper, I meant the next baby.'

The Examination

Preeto took her husband Banta to see a psychiatrist for a checkup.

After examining him, the doctor took Preeto to one side

and said, 'I have some very bad news for you. There is nothing I can do to help your husband. His mind has completely gone.'

'I'm not really surprised,' Preeto replied, 'He's been giving me a piece of it every day for the last twenty years.'

I'm Married...

Santa woke up with a huge hangover after attending his company's New Year's Party. He was not a habitual drinker but kept drinking as the drinks didn't taste like alcohol. He didn't even remember how he got home from the party. As bad as he was feeling, he wondered if he did something wrong. He had to force himself to open his eyes, and the first thing he saw was a couple of Disprins next to a glass of water on the side table.

And, next to them, a red rose!! Santa sat up and finds his clothes in front of him, all clean and pressed. He looks around the room and sees that it is in perfect order, spotlessly clean. So is the rest of the house.

He takes the Disprins, cringes when he sees a huge black eye staring back at him in the bathroom mirror. Then he notices a note from his wife, hanging on the corner of the mirror written in red with little hearts on it and a kiss mark:

'Sweetheart, breakfast is on the table, I left early to get the stuff to make you your favourite dinner tonight. I love you, darling! Love, Preeto.'

He stumbles to the kitchen and sure enough, there is breakfast, steaming hot tea and the newspaper. His son is also at the table, eating.

Santa asks, 'Pappu... what happened last night?'

'Well, you came home after 3.00 a.m., drunk and out of your mind. You fell over the coffee table and broke it, and then you puked in the hallway and got that black eye when you ran into the door.'

Confused, he asked, 'So, why is everything in such perfect order and so clean? I have a rose, and breakfast is on the table waiting for me?'

Pappu replies, 'Oh THAT... Mom dragged you to the bedroom, and when she tried to take your pants off, you screamed.... 'Leave me alone, I'm married!! Leave me alone, I'm married!!'

Banta's Letter to Bill Gates

Bill Gates decided not to invest further in Punjab after receiving a letter from Mr Banta

To: Bill Gates, Microsoft
From: Banta
Date: 1 March 2014
Subject: Problems with my new computer

Dear Mr Bill Gates,
We have bought a computer for our home and we have found some problems, which I want to bring to your notice.
1. There is a 'start' button but there is no 'stop' button. We request you to check this.
2. Is a 're-scooter' available in the system? I find only a 're-cycle', but I own a scooter at my home.
3. There is a 'Find' button which does not work. My wife lost the door key and we tried a lot to trace the key

with this button, but were unable to trace it. Please rectify this problem.

4. My child learnt 'Microsoft Word' now he wants to learn 'Microsoft Sentence'. When will you provide that?

5. I bought computer, CPU, mouse and keyboard, but there is only one icon which shows 'My Computer'. When will you provide the remaining items?

6. It is surprising that Windows says 'My Pictures' but there is not even a single photo of mine. So when will you keep my photo in that.

7. There is 'MICROSOFT OFFICE' but what about 'MICROSOFT HOME' since I use the PC only at home.

8. You provided 'My Recent Documents'. When will you provide 'My Past Documents'?

9. You provided 'My Network Places'. For God's sake please do not provide 'My Secret Places'. I do not want my wife to find out where I go after my office hours.

Last one Mr Bill Gates

P.S: Sir, how is it that your name is Gates but you are selling WINDOWS?

Regards,

Banta

Smartness vs Intelligence

Einstein and Banta are sitting next to each other on a long flight.

Einstein says, 'Let's play a game. I will ask you a question. If you don't know the answer, you pay me only $5 and if I don't know the answer, I will pay you $500.'

Einstein asks the first question: 'What's the distance from the Earth to the Moon?'

Banta doesn't say a word, reaches his pocket and pulls out $5.

Now, it's Banta's turn. He asks Einstein, 'What goes up a hill with three legs and comes down on four legs?'

Einstein searches the net and asks all his smart friends. After an hour, he gives Banta $500.

Einstein going nuts asks, 'Well, so what goes up a hill with three legs and comes down with four?'

Banta reaches his pocket and gives Einstein $5.

Santa's Furniture Business

Santa, a furniture dealer decided that he wanted to expand the line of furniture in his store. So he decided to go to Paris to see what he could find.

After arriving in Paris (this being his first trip ever to the French capital), he met with some manufacturers and finally selected a new range of furniture that he thought would sell well back home in India.

To celebrate the new acquisition, he decided to visit a pub and have a glass of wine. As he sat enjoying his wine, a very beautiful young lady came to his table, asked him something in French (which he did not understand), and gestured towards the chair.

He invited her to sit down. He tried to speak to her in Hindi, Punjabi and English, but she did not speak or know any of these languages. After a couple of minutes of trying to communicate with her, he took a napkin and drew a picture of a wine glass and showed it to her.

She nodded and he ordered a glass of wine for her.

After sitting together at the table for a while, he took another napkin and drew a picture of a plate with food on it and she nodded.

They left the pub and found a quiet cafe that had a small group playing romantic music. They ordered dinner after which he took another napkin and drew a picture of a couple dancing.

She nodded and they got up to dance. They danced until the cafe closed and the band was packing up.

Then, after they were back at their table, the young lady took a napkin and drew a picture of a bed.

Till this day, Santa has no idea how she figured out that he was in the furniture business!

Would You Remarry?

Jeeto: What would you do if I died? Would you get married again?

Santa: Definitely not!

Jeeto: Why not? Don't you like being married?

Santa: Of course I do.

Jeeto: Then why wouldn't you remarry?

Santa: Okay, I'd get married again.

Jeeto: (looking hurt) You would?

Santa: (makes an audible groan).

Jeeto: Would you live in our house?

Santa: Sure, it's a great house.

Jeeto: Would you sleep with her in our bed?

Santa: Where else would we sleep?

Jeeto: Would you let her drive my car?

Santa: Probably, it is almost new.

Jeeto: Would you replace my pictures with hers?

Santa: That would seem like the proper thing to do.

Jeeto: Would you give her my jewellery?

Santa: No, I'm sure she'd want her own.

Jeeto: Would she wear my shoes?

Santa: No, her size is six.

Jeeto: (Silence)

Santa: Shit.

How Do You Like Your Eggs?

Santa and Jeeto got married. Santa thought this would be a modern marriage, which meant equal roles for both partners.

So, the first morning after their honeymoon, Santa brought Jeeto breakfast in bed.

However, Jeeto wasn't impressed with his culinary skills.

She looked disdainfully at the tray, and snorted, 'A poached egg? I wanted scrambled!'

Undaunted, the next morning, Santa brought his true love a scrambled egg.

Jeeto wasn't having any of it. 'Don't you think I like variety? I wanted poached this morning!'

Determined to please his wife, the next morning he brought his true love two eggs: one scrambled and one poached.

'Here, my love. Enjoy!'

Jeeto was furious. 'You idiot, you scrambled the wrong egg!'

Santa at the Magic Door

One Saturday, Santa took his wife and son into to the city for shopping. As they approached town, they were astonished by the sky scrapers.

Santa, never having been to the big city himself, decided to let his wife be at the local mall while he and his son did some sight-seeing.

They entered a large building with an enormous lobby. The son noticed a door on the wall and asked Santa what it was for.

Santa, not knowing, decided to move closer to observe better. A few minutes later, an old lady with a cane came and pressed a button located near the door. The door opened and the old lady entered a small room after which the door shut. Santa and his son are amazed when suddenly the door opened and a very beautiful young lady came out.

Astonished, Santa looked at his son while scratching his head and said, 'Son, I don't know what just happened, but run fast and fetch your mother.'

Missed Call

Santa: A month ago I gave my number to this beautiful lady. She said that she'll call me when she gets back home.

Banta: So, have you got her number yet?

Santa: I haven't received any call from her so far. I think she is homeless!

Health Reasons

Santa: I eat my salad without dressing.

Banta: For health reasons?

Santa: No. Because once hungry who has the time to put on clothes.

Group Chat

Police: Knock Knock!

Santa: Who's there?

Police: Police! Open the door, we only need to talk.

Santa: How many are you?

Police: We are three.

Santa: So why don't you just talk to each other?

Snake Bite

Santa and Banta were hiking in the woods when Santa is bitten on the rear end by a rattlesnake.

'I'll go to town to see a doctor,' Banta says.

He runs for a few miles and reaches a small town where he finds the town's only doctor is busy delivering a baby.

'I can't leave,' the doctor says. 'But here's what to do. Take a knife, cut a little 'x' where the bite is, suck out the poison and spit it on the ground.'

Banta runs back to his friend, who is in agony.

'What did the doctor say?' Santa asks.

'He says you're gonna die.'

Wedding Gift

Santa and Jeeto were at the printers', getting their son's wedding invitations made.

Jeeto was not very good at English so she asked the printer to help her. After the printer had presented her with a draft, she quickly pointed out that the 'RSVP' was missing .

The printer was surprised by Jeeto's knowledge and asked her if she knew what it meant.

Jeeto started to think and after much thought she said, 'Wait! I remember! I remember! RSVP!! It means "Remember, Send Vedding Present!"'

Mental Deficiency

A noted psychiatrist was a guest at a party and his host, Banta, broached the subject in which the doctor was most at ease.

'Would you mind telling me, Doctor,' Banta asked 'how do you detect a mental deficiency in somebody who appears completely normal?'

'It is easy,' he replied. 'You ask him a simple question which everyone should be able to answer without any trouble. If he hesitates, that puts you on the right track.'

'What sort of question?'

'Well, you might ask him, 'Captain Cook made three trips around the world and died during one of them. Which one?'

Banta thought for a moment and then said with a nervous laugh, 'You wouldn't happen to have another example would you? I must confess I don't know much about history.'

Overnight Stay

Having snuck out with a very cute young woman that he met at a party, Banta, exhausted from hours of hot sex, woke up at her apartment at 3.00 a.m.

'Oh God!' Banta thought. 'Jeeto's gonna kill me!'

Trying to figure out how he would explain this to Jeeto without getting whacked with a frying pan, inspiration struck.

Banta dashed out to the nearest pay phone, dialed his home number quickly, and breathlessly said, 'Jeeto, Jeeto! Don't pay the ransom! I escaped!'

Santa's Clients

Santa was in the business of making coats but unfortunately his business was very bad.

One day his partner, Banta, said to him, 'What are we going to do with these fifty coats? They're last year's style and even though we've knocked them down to ₹1,000 each, we still can't sell any.'

Santa replied, 'Use your head, Banta. Price them at ₹2,000 and send five coats each to ten of our best clients. But here's the plan. Put in an invoice for ₹8,000 for only four coats. If I know them, my clients will think we've made a mistake. They'll jump at a bargain and pay ₹8,000.'

'What a terrific idea,' said Banta. 'I'll send them out today.'

Two week later, Banta says to Santa, 'What a stupid idea it was. Every one of those clients returned the parcel and the invoice, but only sent back four coats.'

Wife's Birthday

Santa thought he had conquered his problem of trying to remember his wife's birthday and their anniversary.

He opened an account with a florist, provided that florist with the dates and instructions to send flowers to Jeeto on the appropriate dates along with a note signed, 'Your loving husband.'

Jeeto was thrilled by this new display of attention and all went well until one day, some bouquets later, when Santa came home, kissed her and said offhandedly, 'Nice flowers, where'd you get them?'

Funniest Joke

Once Santa and Banta were travelling along with their friends Monty and Jaggi. Their car was attacked by a band of robbers while on a road surrounded by forests on both sides. Santa and his friends were pulled out of the car. The robbers blasted the car and took Santa and his friends deep into the forest where their boss was waiting.

Now, this boss was fond of jokes. So, he placed a condition that whoever tells a joke that makes every single person present laugh would be left unharmed. But if even one person doesn't laugh, then the teller of the joke would be shot to death.

Banta started telling the funniest joke he had ever heard. 'One day.........' and when he was finished, everybody was rolling with laughter except Santa. So according to the vow, the boss shot poor Banta.

Next, it was Monty's turn. He also narrated the funniest joke he had ever heard. Again everybody laughed but Santa was quiet as a statue. As per the condition, Monty was also shot dead.

Then came Jaggi's turn. As he opened his mouth to tell the joke, Santa suddenly burst into laughter. Everyone was puzzled as Santa was laughing madly.

The boss asked him, 'Why the hell are you laughing without hearing the joke?'

Santa said laughing, 'Oh! Banta's joke was so funny!'

Have an Affair

Banta: All the thrill is gone from my marriage.

Santa: Why not add some spice to your life and have an affair?

Banta: But what if my wife finds out?

Santa: Heck, this is a new age we live in. Go ahead and just tell her about it.

Banta goes home to his wife and says, 'Preeto, I think an affair will help bring us closer.'

'Forget it, I've already tried that. It didn't work,' says Preeto.

Archery Contest

Once upon a time there was an archery contest.

The first archer, wearing a long cape with his face covered, stands in position.

He takes a deep breath and fires an arrow, which finds the center of the target.

Then he removes his cape and screams, 'I am Robin Hood.' The crowd cheers.

The second archer with a cape fires his arrow which hits the center and cuts Robin Hood's arrow into two.

He takes off his cape and screams, 'I am William Tell' and the crowd cheers.

Finally, Santa wearing a cape stands in position. He fires his arrow but it flies past the crowd and kills the chief guest. He takes off his cape and screams, 'I am sorry!'

Banta's Date

Banta called his friend, Santa, and told him that he recently met the woman of his dreams and didn't know what should he do.

Santa said, 'Send her some flowers and an invitation for a home-cooked meal.'

Banta liked the idea and invited the woman.

The following day, Santa called Banta and asked him about the meal.

Banta said, 'It was a flop idea.'

'Didn't the girl come to your house?' asked Banta.

Banta said, 'She did, but she refused to cook!'

Transferring Files

Santa once wanted to transfer some files form one PC to another. These were the steps he followed:

1) Right clicked the mouse on the file which he wanted to

transfer and selected the option 'CUT'.

2) Disconnected the mouse from that PC.

3) Took that mouse carefully and connected it to the other PC where he wanted to copy the file.

4) Right clicked the mouse and selected the 'PASTE' option.

Shitty Santa

Santa and Banta are riding through the desert on their horses. As they ride along, Banta smells something horrible. He stops his horse and turns around.

He says, 'Hey, did you shit in your pants?'

'No,' replies Banta.

He believes him and they keep riding. As they go on, the smell gets worse and flies begin to swarm around them. Banta stops his horse and turns around.

He then says, 'Are you sure you did not shit in your pants?'

'Yes, I am sure,' says Santa.

They keep going and now the smell is becoming unbearable. Santa is swatting the flies away. Banta stops his horse and gets off. He then says, 'Get of your horse and pull down your pants. I thought you said you did not shit in your pants?'

Santa replies, 'I thought you meant today!'

Beautiful Models

Santa and Banta were looking at a catalog and admiring the models.

Santa says to the Banta, 'Have you seen the beautiful girls in this catalog?'

Banta replies, 'Yes, they are very beautiful. And look at the price!'

Santa says, with wide eyes, 'Wow, they aren't very expensive. I'm buying one.'

Banta smiles and pats him on the back, 'Good idea! Order one and if she's as beautiful as she is in the catalog, I will get one too.'

Three weeks later, Banta asks Santa, 'Did you ever receive the girl you ordered from the catalog?'

Santa replies, 'No, but it shouldn't be long now. I got her clothes yesterday!'

Java Interview

Java Interview attended by Banta:

Q. Explain 2-tier and 3-tier Architecture ?

A. Two wheelers like scooters will have 2 tyres and autorickshaws will have 3 tyres.

Q. I want to store more than ten objects in a remote server. Which methodology should be followed?

A. Send it through courier.

Q. Can I modify an object in CORBA?

A. As you wish. I do not have any objections.

Q. How to communicate two threads with each other?

A. Sorry. Non living things can't communicate.

Q. Explain RMI Architecture?

A. I am a computer professional not an architect.

Q. What is the use of Servlets?

A. In hotels, they can replace servers.

Q. What is the difference between Process and Threads?

A. Threads are small ropes. Making a rope from threads is an example of a process.

Q. What is JAR file?

A. File that can be kept inside a jar.

Q. What is JINI?

A. A ghost which was Aladdin's friend.

Q. How will you call an Applet from a Java Script?
A. I will give invitation.
Q. What is bean? Where it can be used?
A. A kind of vegetable which can be used for cooking.
Q. How will you create a binary tree?
A. When we sow a binary seed, a binary tree will grow.

Final Examination

Santa reported for his university final examination which comprised 'Yes/No' type of questions. He takes his seat in the examination hall and stares at the question paper for five minutes. Then in a fit of inspiration, he takes his purse out, removes a coin and starts tossing it, marking the answer sheet: 'Yes' for heads and 'No' for tails.

He is all done within half an hour whereas the rest of the class is sweating it out. During the last few minutes, he is seen desperately flipping the coin, muttering and sweating.

The moderator, alarmed, approaches him and asks what is wrong.

Santa replies, 'I'm rechecking my answers and I don't think I did very good.'

Best Friend

Banta is sitting at the bar furiously downing whiskey shots.

Santa happens to come into the bar and sees him.

'Banta,' says a shocked Santa, 'what are you doing? I've

known you for over fifteen years, and I've never seen you take a drink before. What's going on?'

Without even taking his eyes off his newly filled shot glass, Banta replies, 'My wife just ran off with my best friend.'

He then downs another shot of whisky in one gulp.

'But,' says Santa, 'I'm your best friend!'

Banta turns to Santa, looks at him through bloodshot eyes, smiles, and then slurs, 'Not anymore! He is!'

Misunderstanding

The house owner was delighted with the way Santa had completed all the paintwork on his house.

'You did a great job,' he said as he handed Santa his fees. 'Also, in order to thank you, here's an extra five hundred bucks to take the wife out to dinner and a movie.'

Santa declined, saying, 'No, I can't accept that.'

'I insist,' said the man. 'It would make me very happy if you do it.'

'Well,' said Santa reluctantly, 'If you really don't mind it, I'll do it.'

Later that night, the doorbell rang. Santa was standing outside wearing clean clothes and holding a bouquet of flowers.

Thinking that Santa had forgotten something the house owner asked, 'What's the matter, did you leave something behind?'

'Nope,' replied Santa. 'I'm just here to take the wife out to dinner and a movie like you asked.'

Suicide Bomber

Banta joins a suicide bomber squad and is given a mission to carry out suicide bombings in the enemy camp. His leader straps many bombs to his body and gives him a mobile for communication.

He lands up in the enemy's camp and calls his boss. 'Sir, there are two enemy soldiers here. May I suicide now?'

'No. Wait till you see more soldiers,' says the leader.

After sometime, Banta says, 'Sir now there are twenty-five. May I do it now?'

'Wait for more,' replies his leader.

'Sir, now I am in a midst of hundred soldiers, can I suicide now?' asks Banta

His leader says, 'Yes, go ahead. You will be a martyr. Don't worry about your family. We will look after them.'

Banta pulls his knife and stabs himself in the chest.

Passionate Kisses

Just after a few years of marriage, Banta and his wife Preeto began constantly arguing. Since they had been at each others' throats for some time,they felt that the only way to save their marriage was to try counseling.

'What seems to be the problem?' asked the counsellor

Immediately, Banta hung his face with nothing to say whereas Preeto began describing all the wrongs within their marriage.

After listening to her for a few mintes,, the counsellor went over to her, held her by the shoulders made her stand up, kissed her passionately for several minutes, and sat her back down.

Preeto was speechless. The doctor looked at Banta who was staring in disbelief at what happened.

The counsellor spoke to Banta, 'Your wife needs that at least twice a week!'

Banta scratched his head and replied, 'I can have her here on Wednesdays and Saturdays.'

Free Beer

Banta owned a pub in Ludhiana. During the summer months, a swarm of flies would hover over the buffet table. This had been going on for about a month.

Santa, the neighbourhood mooch, walked in one day.

'I'm not giving you another free beer!' Banta hollered, as he noticed Santa.

Santa, however, was not without a plan. He approached Banta and offered him a deal.

'I've been noticing these flies for the last few weeks. If you'll give me a shot, I'll kill every one of them for you.'

Banta gave him the agreed-upon shot. Once he had downed it, Santa got up and headed for the door.

'All right,' he shouted, 'send them out one at a time!'

Nature Calls

One evening, Banta's driving along the highway when all of a sudden he gets nature's call. He sees a little bar up the way and pulls into the parking lot.

When he gets inside, he finds the place is packed! The bar is crowded with people trying to get drinks, women are dancing and there's hardly any room to stand.

Banta scans the place a couple of times to find the restrooms, but to no avail. Finally, he spots a small stairway and scrambles up.

When he gets to the top, he discovers that all the doors but one are locked. When he opens the door, all he sees is a big hole in the floor. Desperate, he drops his pants and dumps the biggest load he's ever had right there in the hole.

Relieved, he calmly walks down the stairs. The once crowded bar is completely empty, not a soul was in sight. Slowly, a bartender rises from behind the bar.

'What happened?' says Banta.

The bartender responds 'Where were you when the shit hit the fan?!'

Faithful Wife

Santa is talking to Banta about married life.

'You know,' he says, 'I really trust my wife, and I think she has always been faithful to me. But there's always that doubt.'

'Yeah, I know what you mean,' says Banta.

A couple of weeks later, Santa has to go out of town on

a business tour. Before he goes, he gets together with Banta.

'While I'm away, could you do me a favour? Could you watch my house and see if there is anything fishy going on? I mean, I trust my wife but there's always that doubt.'

Banta agrees to help Santa.

Two weeks later Santa comes back and meets Banta. 'So did anything happen?'

'I have some bad news for you,' says Banta.

'The day after you left, I saw a strange car pull up in front of your house. The horn honked and your wife ran out and got into the car and they drove away. Later, after dark, the car came back. I saw your wife and a strange man get out. They went into the house and I saw the light being turned on. I ran over and looked in through the window. Your wife was kissing the man. Then he took off his shirt and then.... they turned off the light.'

'Then what happened?' says Santa.

'I don't know. It was too dark to see.'

'Damn, you see what I mean? There's always that doubt.'

Lost Tourist

A man from Lahore was touring Punjab and got lost. He saw Santa working in his field and stopped for directions.

Santa gave him the necessary directions.

The man wanted to talk a bit so he asked Santa, 'Is this your farm?'

'Yep', said Santa.

'How big is it?' asked the tourist.

'Well, it starts down the road where there is a creek, follows the creek up and over the hill, to about where you can see that big tree. Then it runs across the barn and then down along the fence to the road up that way.'

The tourist smiled and said, 'Well, that's a nice place. Let me tell you about my place in Lahore. I can get into my car and start out from one end of my property just as the sun is coming up in the East. I can drive all-day and just as the sun is setting in the West I reach to other end of my ranch. What do you think of that?'

Santa thought for a second or two, and then said, 'I had a car like that once.'

Car Dents

Banta was driving back from Shimla when there was a terrible hailstorm. Huge hailstones, the size of tennis balls pelted his car leaving it completely dented.

He drove to the nearby automobile centre and asked what should be done. The mechanic explained and said it would cost at least ₹5,000 to repair. Banta said that was too much and asked if there was some other way to fix it.

He decided to have a little fun and said, 'Well you could blow into the tail pipe real hard and they might pop back out.'

Banta decided to give it a try before spending that much money. He drove home and was in the garage with his lips wrapped around the exhaust pipe when his neighbour, Santa, came over to visit.

'What are you doing?' asked Santa.

'I'm blowing into the tailpipe real hard to pop all these dents out of my car,' explained Banta.

'Well silly, it's not going to work,' replied Santa.

'Why not?' asked Banta.

'Because you've got to roll up the windows first.'

Outhouse Hole

Santa and his wife, Jeeto, were living in a farm up in the hills. One day, Santa found that the hole under the outhouse is full. He tells Jeeto that he doesn't know what to do to empty the hole.

Jeeto says, 'Why don't you go ask Banta down the road?'

So, Santa goes down to Banta's house and asks him, 'the hole under my outhouse hole is full, and I don't know how to empty it.'

Banta says, 'Get yourself two sticks of dynamite, one with a short fuse and one with a long fuse. Put them both under the outhouse and light them both at the same time. The first one will go off and shoot the outhouse in the air. While it's in the air the second one will then go off and spread the shit all across your farm, fertilizing your ground. The outhouse should then come back down to the same spot atop the now-empty hole.'

Santa thanks him, then drives to the hardware store and picks up two sticks of dynamite, one with a short fuse and one with a long fuse.

He goes home and puts them under the outhouse. He then lights them and runs behind a tree.

All of a sudden, Jeeto comes running out of the house and into the outhouse! Off goes the first stick of dynamite shooting

the outhouse into the air.

BOOM goes the second stick of dynamite spreading shit all over the farm.

WHAM! The outhouse comes crashing back down atop the hole.

Santa races to the outhouse, throws open the door and asks, 'Jeeto, are you all right?'

As she pulls herself up she says, 'Yeah, but I'm glad I didn't fart in the kitchen.'

Cross-Eyed Bull

Banta had a cross-eyed bull that kept bumping into things. He called up the vet to try to remedy the problem.

The vet said, 'I think the best way is to stick a pipe up his ass and blow real hard so that his eyes straighten out.'

The vet, a seventy-year-old man, inserts a pipe and blows. The bulls' eyes begin to straighten, but the vet soon loses his breath and the bulls' eyes are crossed again. The vet gives it another try, but loses his breath again.

The vet looks at Banta and says, 'You look like a strong man, why don't you give it a try.'

Banta agrees. He then takes the pipe out of the bulls' ass, turns it around, and sticks it back in. He then begins to blow.

'Shit!!!' says the vet. 'Why the hell did you do that for?'

Banta replies, 'You don't think I am going to put my mouth on the same end of the pipe that you had yours on.'

Longer Days

A man was working in a scrap yard during summer vacations at an engineering university.

One afternoon, he was taking apart a piling hammer that had some very large bolts holding it together. One of the nuts had corroded on to the bolt. To loosen it, he started heating the nut with an oxy-acetylene torch.

As he was doing this, one of the dimmest apprentices, Banta, came along. He asked him what he was doing.

The man patiently explained that if he heated the nut, it

would grow larger and release its grip on the bolt so he could then remove it.

'So things get larger when they get hot, do they?' Banta asked.

Suddenly, an idea flashed into his mind, 'Yes,' he said, 'that's why days are longer in summer and shorter in winter.'

There was a long pause and Banta said, 'You know, I always wondered about that,' he said.

Thai Restaurant

Santa and Banta, along with some friends decided to try a Thai restaurant.

While looking at the menu, Banta noticed Santa looking at the vegetarian section of the menu.

'What would you like Santa?' he asked.

'I'm looking at this Eggplant Spicy dish,' Santa replied.

'Santa, you like meat and potatoes. You won't like that dish,' Banta said.

'What do you know,' answered Santa, 'I'm getting it.'

'Santa, I'm telling you, you are a meat and potatoes kind of guy. You won't like it!' Banta exclaimed.

'I'm getting it and that is the last word!' said Santa.

A while later the meals arrive at the table.

Santa looked down at his dish and said to Banta, 'Where are my eggs?'

Santa's Dream

Santa kept having the same dream every night, so he went to consult a doctor.

Doctor: What was your dream about?

Santa: I was being chased by a vampire!

Doctor: (giggles quietly) So... what is the scenery like?

Santa: I was running in a hall way.

Doctor: Then what happened?

Santa: Well that's the weird thing. In every single dream, the same thing happened. I always come to this door, but I can't open it. I keep pushing the door, but it wouldn't budge!

Doctor: Does the door have any letters on it?

Santa: Yes it did.

Doctor: And what did letters spell?

Santa: It said 'Pull'

Fishing License

Banta was carrying a large fish in a bucket of water, caught from a lake, which was well known for its abundant fish, when a Fishery officer stopped him.

'Do you have a fishing license?' asked the officer.

'Don't need a license, this is my pet fish,' said Banta

'Pet fish?' the officer asked.

'Yes, every night I take my fish down to the lake and let him swim around for a while. Then I whistle and he jumps onto the shore and I put him in his bucket and we go back home,' said Banta

'That's nosense. Fish can't do that.'

'You want me to show you?' asked Banta.

'Okay I've got to see this,' said the curious officer.

Banta released the fish into the lake and stood waiting.

'Well?' said the officer after waiting for a few minutes.

'Well, what?' said Banta.

'Are you going to call your fish back?' asked the officer.

'Fish! What fish?' Banta replied.

Banta's Date

A cop stops his patrol car when he sees Banta and his girlfriend sitting on the curb. Banta is lying on his side with his pants pulled down, the girl has her finger inside his butt.

'What the hell is going on?' asks the cop.

The girl says, 'This is my date. When I told him I wouldn't spend the night with him, he started guzzling the booze. Now, he's too drunk to drive me home, so I'm trying to sober him up by making him puke.'

'That's not going to make him puke,' says the cop.

She says, 'Yeah? Wait till I put this finger in his mouth.'

Banta's Delusion

Banta thought he was dead though in reality he was very much alive. His delusion became such a problem that his family finally paid for him to see a psychiatrist.

The psychiatrist spent many laborious sessions trying to convince Banta that he was still alive but nothing seemed to work.

Finally, the doctor tried one last approach. He took out his medical books and proceeded to show Banta that dead men don't bleed. After hours of tedious study, Banta seemed convinced that dead men don't bleed.

'Do you now agree that dead men don't bleed?' the doctor asked.

'Yes, I do,' Banta replied.

'Very well, then,' the doctor said.

He took out a pin and pricked the patient's finger. Out came a trickle of blood.

The doctor asked, 'What does that tell you?'

'Oh my goodness!' Banta exclaimed as he stared incredulously at his finger. 'Dead men do bleed!!'

Santa in ICU

A man was brought in to a hospital's intensive care ward, put on a bed, with tubes coming out everywhere. A week later, another man was admitted in a similar condition.

A few weeks later, one of them had the strength to raise his hand and point to himself and say, 'Bengali.'

The other patient signalled he had heard, raised his own hand, and said, 'Punjabi.'

This act tired them out so badly that it was a week before the first summoned up the strength to say, 'Calcutta.'

The other replied in a frail voice, 'Ludhiana.'

Once more, the strain was too much for them and they passed out. Days passed before the first patient managed to again point to himself and say, 'Asit.'

'Santa,' replied the other.

A few hours later, Asit managed to point to himself again and rasp out weakly, 'Cancer.'

Santa responded, 'Sagittarius.'

A Round of Drinks

Banta was not home at his usual hour, and his wife, Preeto, was fuming, as the clock ticked away. Finally, at about 3.00 a.m, she heard a noise at the front door. As she stood at the top of the stairs, there was Banta, drunk as a fish trying to navigate the stairs.

'Do you realize what time it is?' she asked.

He answered, 'Don't get excited. I'm late because I bought something for the house.'

Immediately her attitude changed, and as she ran down the stairs to meet him halfway, she asked, 'What did you buy for the house, dear?'

'A round of drinks!' said Banta.

My Friend Circle

Santa came home from a secret two year mission only to find his wife, Jeeto, with a new born baby. Furious, he was determined to track down the father to extract revenge.

'Was it my friend, Banta', he demanded.

'No!' his wife replied weeping.

'Was it my friend, Ramta then?' he asked.

'No!' she said, even more upset.

'Well which one of my good for nothing friends did this then?' he asked.

'Don't you think I have any friends of my own?' Jeeto snapped.

Santa's Curtains

Santa enters a store that sells curtains.

'I would like to buy a pair of pink curtains,' he says to the salesman.

The salesman assured him that they had a large selection of pink curtains. He showed him several patterns, but Santa seemed to be having a hard time choosing.

Finally, he selects a lovely pink floral print.

The salesman asks him how many metres of curtain did he need.

'Fifteen inches,' says Santa.

'Fifteen inches? That sounds very small, what room are they for?' asks the salesman.

Santa tells him that they aren't for a room but for his computer monitor.

The surprised salesman replies, 'But, sir, computers do not have curtains!'

'Helllloooooooooo........I've got Windows!'

Umbalo-Gong

Santa and Banta fly to the South Sea islands to study the natives. They go to two adjacent islands and set to work. A few months later Santa takes a boat over to the other island to see how Banta is doing. When he gets there, he finds Banta standing among a group of natives.

'Greetings! How is it going?' says Santa.

'Wonderful!' says Banta, 'I have discovered an important fact about the local language! Watch!'

He points at a palm tree and says, 'What is that?'

The natives, in unison, say, 'Umbalo-gong!'

He then points at a rock and says, 'And that?'

The natives again intone, 'Umbalo-gong!'

'You see!', says Banta beaming. 'They use the same word for rock and for palm tree!'

'That is truly amazing!' says an astonished Santa. 'On the other island, the same word means 'index finger'!'

Crazy Wisdom

Santa is driving past the state mental hospital when his left rear tire suffers a flat. While he is changing the tire, another car goes by, running over the hub cap in which Santa was keeping the lug nuts. The nuts are all knocked into a nearby drain.

Santa is at a loss and is about to go call a cab when he hears a shout from behind the hospital fence, where one of the inmates has been watching the whole thing.

'Hey! Why don't you just take one lug nut off each of the other three wheels? That'll hold your tires on until you can get to a garage or something.'

Santa is startled by the patient's seeming rationality, but realizes the plan will work and installs the spare tire without incident.

Before he leaves, he calls back to the patient. 'You know, that was pretty sharp thinking. Why do they have you in there?'

The patient smiles and says, 'I'm in here because I'm crazy, not because I'm stupid.'

Anniversary Gift

Banta wanted to get his beautiful wife, Preeto, something nice for their first wedding anniversary. So he decided to buy her a cell phone.

He showed her the phone and explained its features.

Preeto simply adored her new phone.

The next day, she was out shopping when her phone rang. To her astonishment, it was Banta on the other end.

'Hi Preeto,' he said, 'how do you like your new phone?'

Preeto replied, 'I just love it! It's so small and your voice is clear as a bell, but there's one thing I don't understand though.'

'What's that, sweetie?' asked Banta.

'How did you know I was at Sukhna Lake?'

Supernatural

At the Intensive Care ward of a hospital, patients always died on the same bed, on Sunday morning at 11.00 a.m., regardless of their medical condition. This puzzled the doctors and some even thought that it had something to do with the supernatural. No one could solve the mystery as to why the deaths took place at 11.00 a.m.

A worldwide expert team was constituted and they decided to go down to the ward to investigate the cause of the incidents. So on the next Sunday morning, few minutes before 11.00 a.m., all the doctors and nurses nervously waited outside the ward to see for themselves what the terrible phenomenon was all about.

Some were holding prayer books and other holy objects to ward off evil.

Just when the clock struck 11.00 a.m., Santa, the part-time sweeper, entered the ward and unplugged the life support system and plugged in the vacuum cleaner.

Awkward Questions!

Since Banta was looking depressed, Santa asked him what was wrong.

'Well,' said Banta, 'I ran afoul of one of those awkward questions women ask. Now I'm in deep trouble at home.'

'What kind of question?' asked Santa.

'My wife asked me if I would still love her when she gets old, fat and wrinkly.'

'That's easy,' said Santa. 'You just say "Of course I will."'

'Yeah,' said Banta, 'that's what I did. Except, I said "Of course I DO..."'

Signature Forgery!

Santa lost his cheque booklet.

He decided to go to the bank after two days to report.

The Bank manager said to him, 'But I warned you to be very careful with your cheque book because anyone can forge your signature.

Santa replied, 'I am not a fool, Sir. I have signed all the cheques already, so, they won't have space to forge my signature!'

Pole Length

Santa and Banta were trying to measure an up-right pole with a yard stick.

'Hey, what are you guys doing?' said a big muscled man.

'We're trying to measure the height of this pole,' replied the duo.

The man wrapped his arms around the pole, pulled it out of the ground, laid it down and measured it. He put it back in the ground and said, '22 feet,' and walked away.

An angry Santa yelled back, 'You idiot we were not trying to see its length. We needed to know its height!'

Fishing

Santa was walking through the Rose Garden in Chandigarh and was astonished to see an old man with a fishing rod in hand, fishing over a beautiful bed of red roses. 'Tsk Tsk!' said Santa to himself. 'What a sad sight. That poor old man is fishing over a bed of flowers. I'll see if I can help.'

So he walked up to the old man and asked, 'What are you doing, my friend?'

'Fishing, Sir.'

'Well how would you like to come have a drink with me?'

The old man stood up, put his rod away and followed the kind stranger to a bar in the corner. He ordered a large glass of Scotch, snacks and a fine cigar.

Santa felt good about helping the old man, and he asked, 'Tell me, old friend, how many did you catch today?'

The old fellow took a long drag on the cigar, blew a careful smoke ring and replied, 'You are the fourth today, Sir!'

Accident Scene

Two guys were speeding down a country road on a motorcycle when the driver slowed down and pulled over.

His leather jacket had a broken zipper and he told his friend, 'I can't drive anymore with the air hitting me in the chest like that.'

'Just put the jacket on backwards,' his friend advised.

They continued down the road but around the next bend, they lost control and crashed.

Banta came upon the accident and ran to call the police.

'Are they showing any signs of life?' asked the police.

'Well,' Banta explained, 'the driver was until I turned his head around the right way!'

An Identity Problem

Santa and Banta were sitting at the bar at Raja Sansi Airport, Amritsar.

'I've come to meet my brother,' said Santa. 'He's due to fly in from Canada in an hour's time. It's his first trip home in forty years.'

'Will you be able to recognize him?' asked Banta.

'I'm sure I won't,' said Santa, 'after all, he's been away for a long time.'

'I wonder if he'll recognize you?' said Banta.

'Of course he will,' said Santa. 'Sure, I haven't been away at all.'

Bus No. 54!

Banta was visiting Delhi for the first time. He wanted to see Palika Bazaar. Unfortunately, he couldn't locate the place, so asked a police officer for directions. 'Excuse me, officer, how do I get to Palika Bazaar?'

The officer replied, 'Wait at this bus stop for bus number fifty-four. It'll take you right there.'

Banta thanked the officer. Three hours later, the police officer returned to the same area and found Banta was still waiting at the bus stop.

The officer got out of his car and said, 'Excuse me, I asked you to wait here for bus number fifty-four to reach Palika Bazaar. That was three hours ago. Why are you still waiting?'

Banta replied, 'Don't worry, officer, it won't be long now. The forty fifth bus just went by!'

Medical Prescription

Santa's father was home after a visit to his doctor. Though usually quite active with his grand-children, this time he was making every effort to avoid them.

Santa notices his dad avoiding the kids and asks him what is wrong.

Immediately, the old man whisks his medicine prescription

out of his pocket and hands it to Santa.

'Read that label. That's why!'

Santa takes the bottle and reads, 'Take two pills a day. KEEP AWAY FROM CHILDREN.'

The Ladies Man

'I'm scared,' Banta said to one of his friends. 'I got a letter from a guy who said he'd break my legs if I didn't stop seeing his wife.'

'Well,' replied his friend, 'I guess you'll have to stop seeing his wife.'

'Easy for you to say.'

'You like her that much?' the friend asks.

'It's not that,' declared Banta. 'He didn't sign his name!'

Medical Students

Two young medical students were standing on a street corner observing people as they passed and discussing any abnormalities that they may have seen in them. They would then attempt to make the correct diagnosis. They spotted Santa leaving a bar waddling like a duck at a slow pace.

The two students introduced themselves to Santa and told him that they didn't agree with each others' diagnosis of his problem.

One says, 'My friend thinks you have a bad case of hemorrhoids, and I think you have a hernia. Which of us is correct?'

Santa replies, 'Well boys, I thought it was a fart, but it looks like we were all wrong!'

Smartest Salesman

Three salesmen were bragging who was the best.

The first said that he was so good that he sold a colour television to a blind man.

The second bragged that he sold a high-tech stereo system to a deaf man.

The third said that he sold a Cuckoo clock to Banta.

The other two asked what was the big deal in that.

The third salesman added, 'Along with the Cuckoo clock, I also sold him fifty kilograms of bird seeds.'

Census Taker

Santa was sitting on his porch, when a man walked up with a pad and pencil in his hand.

'What can I do for you?' Santa asked politely. 'Are you selling something?'

'No, sir, I'm not. I'm a Census Taker,' the man replied.

'A what?' Santa asked, more confused than ever.

'A Census Taker,' he explained. 'We're trying to find out how many people are in India.'

'Well, you're wasting your time here.' Santa answered finally. 'I have no idea.'

Explanation!

Santa wired home that he had been able to wind up his business trip a day early and would be home on Wednesday.

When he walked into his apartment, however, he found his wife, Jeeto, in bed with another man. Furious, he picked up his bag and stormed out. He met his mother-in-law on the street, told her about what had happened and announced that he was filing for divorce in the morning.

'Give my daughter a chance to explain before you do anything,' the older women pleaded.

Reluctantly, he agreed. An hour later, his mother-in-law phoned Santa at his office.

'I knew my daughter would have an explanation,' a note of triumph in her voice. 'She didn't receive your telegram!'

The Inheritance!!

Once Santa and Banta meet on the street. Santa looked dejected and was almost on the verge of tears.

Banta said, 'Hey, how come you look like the whole world caved in?'

Santa said, 'Let me tell you. Three weeks ago, an uncle died and left me fifty lakh.'

'That's not bad.'

'Hold on, I'm just getting started. Two weeks ago, a cousin I never knew died and left me twenty lakh.'

'I'd like that.'

'Last week, my grandfather passed away. I inherited almost a million.'

'The how come you look so glum?'

'This week—nothing!'

Black Coffee

Santa and Banta went into a diner that looked as though it had seen better days. As they slid in to a booth, Banta wiped some crumbs from the seat. Then he took a napkin and wiped some moisture from the table. The waitress came over and asked if they would like to look at the menu.

'No thanks,' said Santa. 'I'll just have a cup of black coffee.'

'I'll have black coffee too,' Banta said. 'And please make sure the cup is clean.'

The waitress shot him a nasty look. She turned and marched off in to the kitchen. Two minutes later, she was back.

'Two cups of black coffee,' she announced. 'Which one of you wanted the clean cup?'

Fastest Worker

Santa got a part time job at the Chandigarh Post Office. The first assignment his supervisor gave him was the job of sorting the mail.

Santa separated the letters so fast that his movements were literally a blur. Extremely pleased by this, the supervisor approached Santa at the end of his first day.

'I just want you to know,' the supervisor said, 'that I'm very pleased with the job you did today. You're one of the fastest workers we've ever had.'

'Thank you, Sir' said Santa, beaming, 'and tomorrow I'll try to do even better.'

'Better?' the supervisor asked with astonishment. 'How can you possibly do any better than you did today?'

Santa replied, 'Tomorrow I'm going to read the addresses.'

Overturned Wagon

Pappu, Santa's son, accidentally overturned his wagon load of corn. The farmer who lived nearby heard the noise.

'Hey Pappu!!' the farmer yelled. 'Forget your troubles. Come in with us. Then I'll help you get the wagon up.'

'That's mighty nice of you,' Pappu answered, 'but I don't think my father would like me to.'

'Aw, come on,' the farmer insisted.

© santabanta.com

'Well okay,' he finally agreed, and added, 'But my father won't like it.'

After a hearty lunch, Pappu thanked his host. 'I feel a lot better now, but I know dad is going to be real upset.'

'Don't be foolish!' the farmer said with a smile. 'By the way, where is he?'

'Under the wagon.'

The Route to Heaven!

Three men: a philosopher, a mathematician and Santa, were inside a car when it crashed into a tree. Before anyone knew, the three men found themselves standing before the Pearly Gates of Heaven, in the presence of St Peter and the Devil.

'Gentlemen,' the Devil started, 'Since Heaven is becoming overcrowded, St Peter has decided to limit the number of people entering Heaven. If either of you can ask me a question, for which I don't have an answer, then you're worthy enough to go to Heaven. Else, you'll come with me to Hell.'

The philosopher then stepped up. 'Okay, give me the most comprehensive report on Socrates' teachings.' With a snap of his finger, a stack of paper appeared next to the Devil. The philosopher read it and concluded it was correct. 'You go to Hell!' and with another snap of the finger, the philosopher disappeared.

The mathematician then asked, 'Give me the most complicated formula you can ever think of.' With a snap of his finger, another stack of paper appeared. The mathematician read it and reluctantly agreed it was correct.

'You also go to Hell!' and with another snap of the finger,

the mathematician too disappeared.

Next, Santa stepped forward and said, 'Bring me a chair.' The Devil brought forward a chair. 'Drill seven holes on the seat.' The Devil did as told. Santa then sat on the chair and let out a very loud fart. Standing up, he asked, 'Which hole did my fart come out from?'

The Devil inspected the seat and said, 'The third hole from the right.' 'Wrong,' said Santa. 'It came out from my asshole.'

Santa went to Heaven.

Body Odour

It was a really hot day at the office. There were about twenty people in close quarters and everyone was sweating, even with the fan on.

All of a sudden, people started to wrinkle their noses at an odour passing through the air. It was the most hideous smell anyone had ever smelt.

One man said, 'Uh oh, someone's deodorant isn't working.'

Santa replied from the distant corner, 'It can't be me. I'm not wearing any.'

Adoption!

Santa and Jeeto were delighted when their long wait to adopt a baby came to an end when the adoption centre called and told them that there was a wonderful Tamil baby boy. The couple took him without hesitation.

On their way home from the adoption centre, they stopped by the local college so they could enroll in night courses.

After they filled out the forms, the registration clerk inquired, 'What ever possessed you to study Tamil?'

Santa and Jeeto said proudly, 'We just adopted a Tamil baby, and in a year or so he'll start to talk. We just want to be able to understand him.'

Speech Impediment

Santa and Banta were enjoying a few drinks down at the local bar, when Santa said to Banta, 'If I ask you a question, will you promise to answer me honestly?'

'Yeah, sure thing,' replied his friend, 'fire away.'

'Well,' said Santa, 'why do you think all the guys around here find my wife so attractive?'

'It's probably because of her speech impediment,' replied Banta.

'What do you mean her speech impediment?' inquired Santa. 'My wife doesn't have a speech impediment!'

'Well,' replied Banta, 'you must be the only guy who hasn't noticed that she can't say "NO"!'

Gastric Problem!

Banta was delighted to finally be invited home to meet the parents of the young woman he'd been seeing for some time.

He was quite nervous and by the time he arrived at the

doorstep, he began experiencing gastric distress.

The problem developed into acute flatulence, and halfway through coffee, Banta realised he couldn't hold it any longer without exploding. A tiny fart escaped.

'Boxer!' called out the young woman's mother to the family dog, lying at Banta's feet.

Relieved at the dog having been blamed, Banta let out another, slightly larger one.

'Boxer!' she called out sharply.

One more and I'll feel fine thought Banta to himself

This time he let out a really big one.

'Boxer!' shrieked the mother. 'Get over here before he shits on you!'

Lottery!

Santa finds himself in serious financial trouble as his business has gone bust. He is so desperate that he decides to ask Bhagwan for help. He goes to a temple and begins to pray.

'Oh Bhagwan, please help me, my business is ruined and if I do not get some money, I am going to lose my house as well. Please let me win the lottery.'

Lottery night comes and somebody else wins it. Santa goes back to the temple.

'Bhagwan, please let me win this time, I have lost my business, my house and I am going to lose my car as well.'

Lottery night comes and Santa still has no luck.

'Bhagwan, why have you forsaken me? I have lost my business, my house, my car and my wife and children are starving. I do not ask your for help often and I have always been a good servant to you. Why won't you just let me win the lottery this one time so I can get my life back in order?'

Suddenly there is a blinding flash of light as the sky parts and Santa is confronted by the voice of Lord:

'SANTA, BUY THE DAMN TICKET FIRST.'

Mystery!

Santa happened to participate in the shortest story writing competition.

The organizers had put a condition that the story must have four themes: religion, sex, suspense and mystery.Santa's story was of one sentence long and read 'Oh God, my wife is going to deliver a child'.

Ostensibly amused, the organizers asked the judged whether it contained all the four ingredients! The judge replied affirmatively and gave his explanation as below:

Oh God: religion.

My wife: sex.

Going to deliver a child: suspense (a girl or a boy?)

'Okay.... but where is the mystery?' asked one of the organizers.

Santa replied, 'who is the father?'

He was declared the winner for writing the shortest story!

Biggest Jerks!

Banta was sitting at the table, reading the newspaper after breakfast. He came across an article about a beautiful actress who was going to marry a football player who was known for his lack of IQ and common knowledge.

Banta turned to his wife with a questioning look on his face. 'I'll never understand why the biggest jerks get the most attractive wives.'

His wife replies, 'Why thank you, dear!'

Day Off!

Banta goes to see his supervisor in the front office.

'Sir,' he says, 'we're doing some heavy house-cleaning at home tomorrow, and my wife, Preeto, needs me to help with moving and hauling stuff from top floor and the garage.'

'We're short-handed, Banta,' the boss replies. 'I can't give you the day off.'

'Thanks, Sir,' says Banta, 'I knew I could count on you!'

Redline Bus!

Banta showed his palm to a palmist.

He examined the lines on Banta's hand and said, 'A beautiful girl will come into your life, but be very careful.'

'Why do I have to be careful?' Banta retorted. 'She should be careful. I drive a Redline bus!'

Painful Pinch!

As the crowded elevator descended, Banta's wife, Preeto, became increasingly furious with Banta, who was delighted to be pressed against a gorgeous girl.

As the elevator stopped at the main floor, the girl suddenly turned, slapped Banta, and said, 'That will teach you to pinch!'

Bewildered, Banta was halfway to the parking lot with Preeto when he choked, 'I... I... didn't pinch that girl.'

'Of course you didn't,' said Preeto, consolingly, 'I did.'

Rooster Replacement

Banta was driving down a quiet country lane when a rooster strayed out into the road. Smack! The rooster disappeared under the car and a bunch of feathers were floating in the air.

Shaken, Banta pulled over at the farmhouse, rang the doorbell. A farmer appeared.

Banta, said nervously, 'I think I killed your rooster. Please allow me to replace him.'

'Suit yourself,' the farmer replied, 'you can go join the other chickens that are around the back.'

About Half Past Four!

Santa goes to the doctor complaining of hearing loss.

The doctor examines him and says he would recommend a new hearing aid. 'This is the finest hearing aid being manufactured now. I wear one myself,' says the doctor.

'What kind is it?' asks the Santa.

'About half past four!' replies the doctor.

Accident!

Santa and Banta were driving in from the opposite directions when their cars met with a head-on collision. They were able to get out of their cars without any serious injury, but the cars were totalled.

Before Santa could say anything, Banta said, 'Instead of fighting over whose fault it was, why don't we just celebrate that we were able to come out alive?'

Santa said, 'Yeah, good idea!'

'I have a bottle of whisky in the trunk. Why don't I pull that out?' suggested Banta. He went around, and luckily the bottle was not damaged in the accident.

He gave it to Santa and said, 'Here, drink some!'

Santa took the bottle and chugged half of it down. Then he wiped his mouth and handed the bottle over to Banta.

'Here, you have some!'

Banta passed it back and said, 'No, I think I'll wait till the police gets here.'

Motion Sickness

Santa and Banta are discussing the possibility of love. 'I thought I was in love three times,' Santa says.

'Thought...?' Banta asks. 'What do you mean?'

'Three years ago, I cared very deeply for a woman who wanted nothing to do with me,' Santa says.

'Wasn't that love?' Banta asks.

'No, that was obsession,' Santa explains. 'Then two years ago, I cared very deeply for an attractive woman who didn't understand me.'

'Wasn't that love?' asks Banta.

'No, that was lust,' Santa replies. 'And just last year, I met a woman while I was on a cruise. She was gorgeous, intelligent, a great conversationalist and had a super sense of humour. Whenever I followed her on that ship, I would get a very strange sensation in the pit of my stomach.'

'Well, wasn't that love,' asks Banta.

'No. That was motion sickness!' Santa replies.

Ouststanding!

A man is driving down a country road, when he spots Santa standing in the middle of a huge field, doing nothing.

He pulls the car over to the side of the road and walks towards Santa. 'Ah excuse me sir, but what are you doing?' asks the man.

Santa replies, 'I'm trying to win a Nobel Prize.'

'How?' asks the man, puzzled.

'Well I heard they give the Nobel Prize to people who are outstanding in their field.'

Jumping Santa

Santa was asked to try out a new parachute with a radio link to a guy on the ground who would say when to pull the release cord for the parachute.

Santa jumped out of the plane and started to fall. When he reached a thousand feet, the guy on the ground said, 'okay pull the release cord now.' Santa didn't take any notice and kept falling.

He got down to 500 feet and the guy on the ground said, 'quick pull the cord. You are getting close,' but Santa just ignored him and kept falling.

He got down to 100 feet and the guy on the ground said 'quick pull the cord.' Santa still ignored him.

He got down to 10 feet, the guy on the ground said, 'this is your last chance you'll be killed if you don't pull the cord now.'

Santa replied, 'That is okay. I can jump from here!'

Judicious Decision

Taking his seat in his chambers, the judge faced the opposing lawyers, Santa and Banta.

'So,' he said, 'I have been presented with a bribe by both of you.'

Both, Santa and Banta squirmed uncomfortably.

'You, advocate Santa, gave me ₹60,000. And you, advocate Banta, gave me ₹50,000.'

The judge reached into his pocket and pulled out a cheque.

He handed it to Santa, and stated, 'Now, I'm returning ₹10,000, and we're going to decide this case strictly on its merits.'

Memories of Santa

A minister visited an asylum for the mentally disturbed women and was taken on a tour of the facilities by one of the doctors. Walking down the dismal, echoing corridors, the minister was troubled by the cries and groans of the patients coming from their rooms.

'I hope that I can be of some help and comfort to these poor souls,' he told his guide.

The doctor stopped at a door and they looked through the small window.

'This is a sad case,' said the doctor.

The patient rocked back and forth on her cot, sobbing and sighing, 'Santa,' she repeated over and over. 'Oh, Santa!'

'She was to marry a man named Santa,' said the doctor. 'And on their wedding day Santa ran off with another woman. It broke her heart and she went mad.'

They moved on to another door and looked in. Inside the patient was bound in a straight-jacket, shrieking insanely, 'Santa! Santa!'

'Let me guess,' said the minister. 'She lost Santa also.'

'No,' answered the doctor. 'She's the one that got him!'

Fishy!

Santa and Banta were coming up in an inlet in their motor boat when they saw another boat loaded with fish.

Seeing how their luck had been awful, Santa asked the fisherman what his secret was.

The fisherman replied, 'Just go out to sea till the water is fresh. Then stop there and drop your line. You will get a huge haul of fish!'

Excited, Santa fired up the motor and headed out to sea. When they got a little ahead, he told Banta to fill up a bucket and taste the water.

Banta complied and said, 'It is salty, not fresh!'

So Santa went further out and told Banta to taste the water again after some time.

Banta replied, 'It is still salty!' And so, they kept going further into the sea. This went on for hours and every time Banta replied that the water was salty. Finally, it was starting to get dark and they were in the middle of nowhere, when Santa

asked Banta to taste the water one last time.

Banta replied, 'But Santa, there is no more water left in the bucket.

While Driving!

Banta's friend from a foreign country visited India for the first time.

He asked Banta tips for safe driving on the Indian roads as he wished to go for a sight-seeing tour in his own car.

'While driving, if you come across a roadways bus, just slow down and let it pass. If a truck approaches you, pull your vehicle to the side and start again only when it has passed. But if you see a Fauji truck approaching you, stop your car on the side track, get out of it and climb a nearby tree,' advised Banta.

Collateral?

Santa applied for a loan of ₹10,00,000.

The banker pulled out the loan application, 'What have you got for collateral?'

'What's collateral?'

'Well that's something of value that would cover the cost of the loan. Have you got any vehicle?'

'Yes, a Tata Sumo.'

The banker shook his head. 'Any fixed assets, like land, house, building?'

'Yes, I have five acres of land and a small farm house.'

Finally, the banker decided to offer the loan.

Several weeks later, Santa was back in the bank. He then handed the banker the money to pay his loan off.

'What are you going to do with the rest of that money?'

'Don't know.'

'Why don't you deposit it in my bank,' he asked.

'What is deposit.'

'You put the money in our bank and we take care of it for you. When you want to use it, you can withdraw it.'

Santa leaned across the desk and asked, 'What have you got for collateral?'

Wrong Bus!

Santa and Banta are walking home drunk. They've no money to get a taxi and are staggering all over the place when they find themselves outside the bus depot.

Santa has a brainwave and says to Banta, 'Get in there and steal a bus so we can drive home and I'll stay out here and look out for the police'.

Banta breaks into the garage and is gone for twenty minutes while Santa is wondering what the hell he's doing.

Eventually, Santa sticks his head around the door and sees Banta running from bus to bus and looking very worried.

'What the hell are you doing, get a move on!'

Banta replies, 'I can't find a number 25B anywhere'.

Whereupon Santa, holding his hands to his head in disbelief, shouts, 'You idiot, steal a number 27 and we'll get off at the roundabout and walk the rest of the way!'

Santa's Closet!

Santa came home earlier than usual, when his wife, Jeeto's lover was still in the apartment. She hid her lover in a closet, and served dinner. As they ate, something rustled in the closet.

'What's that?' Santa asked.

'Nothing, darling. Just jackets.'

After a while, they again heard some noise in the closet.

'What the hell is that?'

'I'm telling you, just jackets.'

A few minutes later, the noise came once more.

'I'll check it,' Santa said. 'You'll regret it if it's not jackets.'

Santa yanked the closet's door open. Inside, he saw a man who held a pistol. Santa quietly closed the door and said, 'Indeed, jackets, darling.'

Thumb Wipe!

Banta was driving down the street looking for a place to stop so he could go to the bathroom. He stopped at a bar and went inside.

'Bartender! Where is the bathroom, I really need to go?!' he said.

The bartender pointed to the bathroom. Banta went in and looked over to the side. There was no toilet paper!

'Oh no!'

He looked over again and saw a sign that said: If out of toilet paper use your thumb and ask the bartender for a 'thumb wipe'.

'Bartender!' he said.

'What can I do for you?' asked the bartender.

'There is no toilet paper and I need a thumb wipe.'

'Oh,' said the bartender. 'Put your thumb on the bar.'

'On the bar?'

The bartender replied, 'Yes, on the bar.'

So Banta put his thumb on the bar and the bartender pulled out a hammer and slammed it hard on Banta's thumb.

Banta's instant reaction was to put his thumb in his mouth.

.

Kicking Mule!

Santa and Banta had a mule that worked very hard. The only problem was every time they went to put the mule back in his stall, his ears would brush the top of the entrance and he would go nuts and kick everything.

One day, Santa and Banta decided to cut an opening in the top to prevent the mule's ears from grazing against it. While they were working, a neighbour stopped by and asked what they were doing, so they explained the problem. The neighbour suggested that they could save a lot of work and time if they simply took a shovel and dug the entrance down a little bit. They thanked their neighbour. Then Santa said to Banta, 'Some stupid neighbour we have, it's not his feet that's too long, it's his ears!'

Vacuum Cleaner!

An old lady answered a knock at her door, only to be confronted by Banta, carrying a vacuum cleaner.

'Good morning', said Banta. 'If I could take a couple of minutes of your time, I would like to demonstrate the very latest in high powered vacuum cleaners.'

'Go away!' said the old lady. 'I haven't got any money!'

And she proceeded to close the door. Quick as a flash, Banta wedged his foot in the door and pushed it wide open.

'Don't be too hasty!', he said. 'Not until you have at least seen my demonstration.'

And with that, he emptied a bucket of horse manure onto her hallway carpet.

'If this vacuum cleaner does not remove all traces of this horse manure from your carpet, Madam, I will personally eat the remainder.'

'Well,' she said, 'I hope you've got a damned good appetite, because the electricity was cut off this morning.'

Banta's Faith

Banta was walking in the mountains enjoying the scenery when he stepped too close to the edge of the mountain and started to fall.

In desperation he reached out and grabbed the branch of an old tree hanging onto the side of the cliff. Full of fear he assessed his situation.

He was about 100 feet down a cliff and about 900 feet

from the floor of the canyon below. If he should slip again he'd plummet to his death.

Full of fear, Banta cries out, 'Help me!' But there was no answer.

He cried out repeatedly but to no avail.

Finally, Banta yelled, 'Is anybody up there? '

A deep voice replied, 'Yes, I'm up here.'

'Who said that?'

'It's God.'

'Can you help me?'

'Yes, I can help. Have faith in me.'

'Help me!'

'Just let go.'

Looking around, Banta became full of panic. 'What?'

'Have faith in me. Let go. I will catch you.'

'Uh...is there anybody else up there?'

Who's Who

A group of loud and rowdy drunks were making a racket on the street in the wee hours of the morning. The lady of the house flung open a window and shouted at them to keep quiet.

'Is this where Banta lives?' one of the drunks asked.

'Yes, it is,' the woman replied.

'Well then,' said the drunk, 'Could you come and take him back so the rest of us can go home?'

Who's Fastest!

Santa's son and two of his friends were heading home from school one day when one of them started the time-honoured game of paternal one-upmanship.

He said, 'My dad's way faster than any of yours. He can throw a fast ball at 90-kmph, run and catch it just after it crosses the wickets at the striker's end!'

The second boy said, 'Oh yeah? Well, my dad can shoot a bullet from his gun and run to the target and hold it up to make sure the bullet hits the bull's eye!'

Santa's son said, 'Your dads don't even come close mine in terms of speed. My dad works for the government, and even though he works every day until 5.00 p.m. he gets home at 4.00 p.m.!'

Overweight Dog

Santa took his dog to the vet for its annual check-up.

'Your dog is overweight,' the vet said. 'You should cut back on his food a little and make sure he gets some exercise. Try playing fetch with him.'

'That's impossible,' Santa replied. 'I can't play fetch with my dog.'

'Why not?' asked the puzzled vet.

'Because,' Santa said, 'he can't throw.'

Government's Jawai (son-in-law)!

Banta was a Government Employee. One day, out of boredom, he decides to see what's in his old filing cabinet. He pokes through the contents and comes across an old brass lamp.

'This will look nice on my mantelpiece,' he decides and takes it home with him.

While polishing the lamp, a genie appears and grants him three wishes.

'I wish for a beautiful Castle right now!'

He gets one. Now that he can think more clearly, he states his second wish.

'I wish to be on an island where beautiful women reside.'

Suddenly he is on an island with gorgeous females eyeing him lustfully.

He tells the genie his third and last wish, 'I wish I'd never have to work ever again.'

OOPS! He's back in his office again.

Installing Poles!

A supervisor sent out two groups of men to put up telephone poles along a new highway and asked them to report at the end of the day.

The men were gone all day and returned just as the sun was setting.

The supervisor asked the leader of the first group how many poles they had installed.

The reply was eleven.

He patted the guy on the back and said, 'Not bad.'

Then he went to Santa, leader of the second group, and asked him the same question.

'Two,' said Santa.

'Two! All you installed were two?!The other group installed eleven!' The supervisor exclaimed angrily.

'Yeah,' Santa answered, 'But you should have seen how many they left sticking out!'

Old Ghost!

Santa and Banta left the bar after a long night of drinking, jumped into their car and were on their way. After a couple of minutes, an old man appeared on the passenger window and tapped lightly. Banta screamed, 'Look at the window. There's an old ghost's face here!'

Santa sped, but the old man's face stayed at the window. Scared out of his wits, Banta rolled his window and said, 'What do you want?'

The old man softly replied, 'You got any tobacco?'

Banta handed the old man a cigarette, rolled up his window in terror and yelled to Santa, 'Step on it.'

A few minutes later they calmed down and started laughing again.

Santa said, 'I don't know what happened, but don't worry; the speedometer says we're doing eighty now.'

All of a sudden, there was a light tapping on the window and the old man reappeared.

'There he is again,' Banta yelled. He rolled down the window and said shakily, 'Yes?'

'Do you have a light?' the old man quietly asked.

Banta threw a lighter out the window saying, 'Step on it!'

They were driving about hundred miles an hour, trying to forget what they had just seen and heard, when all of a sudden there was some more tapping.

'Oh my God! He's back!'

Banta rolled down the window and screamed in stark terror, 'WHAT NOW?'

The old man gently replied, 'You want some help getting out of the mud?'

Toilet Brush!

Banta and his colleagues were at work one day when they decided to get in on the weekly raffle. They bought tickets, seeing it was for charity.

The following week, when the raffle was drawn, they each won a prize.

His colleague, who won the first prize, got six month's supply of Cadbury's chocolates.

Second prize winner got three month's supply of Cadbury's chocolates.

Banta won the tenth prize—a toilet brush.

About a week later, at the office canteen, the first prize winner asked the others how they were enjoying their prizes.

'Great,' said the second prize winner. 'I love chocolates'

'So do I,' said the first prize winner. 'And how's the toilet brush?' he asked Banta

'Not so good,' Banta said, 'I think I'll go back to paper.'

Hired to Worry!

Fresh out of business school, a young man applied for the post of an accountant. He was being interviewed by a very nervous Banta, who ran a small business.

'I need someone with an accounting degree,' Banta said. 'But mainly, I'm looking for someone to do my worrying for me.'

'Excuse me?' said the baffled accountant.

'I worry about a lot of things,' Banta said. 'But I don't want to have to worry about money. Your job will be to take all the money worries off my back.'

'I see,' said the accountant. 'And how much does the job pay?'

'I'll start you at eighty thousand.'

'Eighty thousand dollars!' the accountant exclaimed. 'How can such a small business afford a sum like that?'

'That,' said Banta, 'is your first worry.'

The Coolest One!

Three friends Santa, Banta and Jugnu were in Shimla. Once, while they were at a local bar, they got talking about how cold it was outside, and how cold their houses were. They could agree on everything except whose house was the coldest. They decided to find out for themselves.

They went to Jugnu's house. Jugnu flung a glass of water into the air. The water froze in mid-air and fell onto the floor as ice.

'Not bad', said Santa and Banta.

Next they went to Banta's place. Banta took a big breath

and exhaled, whereupon his breath froze into a big lump and fell on the floor.

'Wow, that's colder than mine!' said Jugnu.

But Santa exclaimed that his house was the coldest and off they went to Santa's place.

Santa went into the bedroom, threw back the thick furs, and retrieved one of the several small balls of ice. He put it on a spoon and held it over a match.

When it heated up enough, it went 'FFFAAAARRRRTTT'.

Refilling!

Santa and Banta had to get across the desert. Since they didn't have enough money to hire a car, they decided to buy a camel.

The camel dealer promised them that the camel would get them across the desert if they made sure he was full of water before they left.

They took the camel down to the water hole, but the camel would not drink.

'I have an idea. Why don't I hold his head down in the water and you suck on his butt. That way the water will be drawn up into him like a straw, 'said Santa.

Banta thought about this for a while and finally agreed.

After a while Santa asked, 'Well is it working?'

Banta replied, 'I think it is going to work, but you have to hold his head up a little because I'm only getting mud.'

Special Offer!

Santa goes into the dentist's office to get a bad tooth pulled out. As he opens his mouth and the dentist is about to drill, he asks how long would the procedure take.

'You'll be out of here before you know it, and won't feel a thing. The anesthesia will last ten minutes.'

'And how much will this cost? asked Santa.

'Five hundred rupees,' the dentist said plainly.

'Yeesh!!!,' Santa grumbled, 'it's a crime to hold a man captive for five minutes and charge him five hundred bucks!'

'I shall offer you a special discount,' the dentist said at which, Santa was pleasantly relieved.

'I'll take fifteen minutes to do the extraction.'

Speeding!

Banta was quite inventive and was always trying out new things. One day he thought he'd see just how fast a bicycle could go before it became uncontrollable. He asked his friend, who owned an old Maruti, if he could tie his bike to the bumper of his car to test his theory.

'Sure,' said his friend.

So Banta tied his bike to the back of the car and said to his friend, 'I'll ring my bike bell once, if I want you to go faster, twice, if I want you maintain the speed, and repeatedly if I want you to slow down.' Things were going pretty well, with the car driver slowly speeding up to well over 60 kmph. Banta was handling the speed just fine. But, all of sudden, a black Honda came up beside them and before they knew it, the man driving the Maruti forgot all about Banta and his bicycle and took to racing with the Honda.

Further down the road sat Officer Santa in his police cruiser with his radar gun. He heard the two cars before his radar flashed 100 kmph.

He called the headquarters on his radio, 'Hey, you guys aren't going to believe this, but there's a Honda and a Maruti racing out here on Highway 22, and there's a guy on a cycle ringing his bell and waving his arms trying to pass them!'

Mystery-lover!

Banta, a mystery-lover takes his place in the theater for the opening night, but his seat is way back..

Banta calls an usher over and whispers, 'I just love a good mystery and I have been anxiously anticipating the opening of this show. However, in order to carefully follow the clues and fully enjoy the play, I have to watch a mystery close up. Look how far away I am! If you can get me a better seat, I'll give you a handsome tip.'

The usher nods and says he would be back shortly.

Looking forward to a large tip, he speaks with his co-workers in the box office, hoping to find some closer seats. With just three minutes left until curtain, he finds an unused ticket near the ticket window and snatches it up.

Returning to Santa, he whispers, 'follow me.'

The usher leads him down to the second row, and proudly points out the empty seat right in the middle.

'Thanks so much,' said Banta, 'This seat is perfect.'

He then hands the usher a quarter.

The usher looks down at the quarter, leans over and whispers, 'The butler did it in the parlour with the candlestick.'

Chronic Disease!

An army Major visiting the sick army men went to one soldier and asked, 'What's your problem, Soldier?'

'Chronic syphilis, Sir.'

'What treatment are you getting?'

'Five minutes with the wire brush each day.'

'What's your ambition?'

'To get back to the front, Sir.'

'Good man,' said the Major.

He went to the next bed. 'What's your problem, Soldier?'

'Chronic piles, Sir.'

'What treatment are you getting?'

'Five minutes with the wire brush each day.'

'What's your ambition?'

'To get back to the front, Sir.'

'Good man,' barked the Major.

He moved to the next bed where Santa was lying and asked, 'What's your problem, Soldier?'

'Chronic gum disease, Sir'

'What treatment are you getting?'

'Five minutes with the wire brush each day.'

'What's your ambition?'

'To get the wire brush before the other two, Sir!'

Chocolate Peanuts!

Santa visits his aunt in the nursing home. It turns out that she is taking a nap, so he just sits down in a chair in her room, flips through a few magazines and munches on some peanuts kept in a bowl on the table.

Eventually, the aunt wakes up and Santa realizes that he had absentmindedly finished the entire bowl.

'I'm so sorry, auntie, I've eaten all of your peanuts!'

'That's okay, dearie,' the aunt replied. 'After I've sucked the chocolate off, I don't care for them anyway.'

Santa's New Car

Santa had just gotten a new car and was out for a drive when he accidentally cut off a truck driver. The truck driver motioned for Santa to pull over.

When Santa did, he got out of his truck and pulled a piece of chalk from his pocket. He drew a circle on the side of the road and gruffly commanded to Santa, 'Stand in that circle and DON'T MOVE!'

He then went to Santa's car and cut up his leather seats.

When he turned around, Santa had a slight grin on his face, so he said, 'Oh you think that's funny? Watch this!'

He gets a bat out of his truck and breaks every window in Santa's car. When he turns and looks at Santa, he still has a smile on his face.

The truck driver is getting really mad. He gets his knife back out and punctures all the tires.

Now Santa's laughing.

The truck driver is really starting to lose it. He goes back to his truck and gets a can of petrol, pours it on Santa's car and sets it on fire.

He turns around and Santa is laughing so hard he is about to fall down.

'What's so funny?' the truck driver asked Santa.

Santa replied, 'Every time you weren't looking, I stepped outside the circle.'

Quick Thinking!

Santa used to work in a saw-mill. He was in hospital after he lost his arm in an accident. Banta was visiting him in the hospital.

'It was really bad that you lost your hand. However thank God that it was your left hand, since you are right-handed,' said Banta.

'It is also because of my quick thinking. Actually it was the right hand which was going to be caught in the machine. Then I realised that I am right-handed and so switched hands just in time!' said Santa.

Who's the Boss?

A retiring farmer needed to rid his farm of animals in preparation for selling his land, so he went to every house in his village.

He gave a horse to the houses where the husband was the boss and a chicken to the houses where the wife was the boss.

When the farmer arrived at the end of the street, he met Banta and Preeto, who were outside gardening.

'Who's the boss around here?' he asked.

'I am,' replied Banta. 'Well, then, I have a black horse and a brown horse,' the farmer said.

'Which one would you like?'

Banta thought for a minute and said, 'The black one...'

'No, no, no... the brown one,' interrupted Preeto.

The farmer shook his head and remarked to Banta, 'Here's your chicken.'

Alternate Sport!

Santa and Banta met at the club for their weekly golf game.

And for the third week in a row, it was raining hard.

Banta: Well, Santa, what do you want to do now?

Santa: Badminton?

Banta: Nah.

Santa: Shoot some pool?

Banta: Nah.

Santa: Cards?

Banta: Nah. Hey, I've got an idea. We can go over to my house and fool around with my wife, Preeto.

Santa: What do you mean?

Banta: Just what I said. We'll go to my house and fool around with my wife.

Santa: What about me?

Banta: She's a sport. She won't mind at all.

Santa: Well… if you think it's okay…

At Banta's house

Banta: Preeto, I'm home. Sweetheart! Damn! She must have gone shopping. Tell you what, Santa, Let's go to your house!

Smart Santa

A man with no arms walked up to a bar and asked for a beer.

Santa, the bartender, shoved the foaming glass in front of him.

'Look,' said the customer, 'I have no arms. Would you please hold the glass up to my mouth?'

'Sure', said Santa and did what was asked.

'Now,' said the customer, 'I wonder if you'd be so kind as to get my handkerchief out of my pocket and wipe the foam off my mouth.'

'Certainly.' And it was done.

'If,' said the armless man, 'you'd reach in my right hand pants pocket, you'll find the money for the beer.'

Santa got the money from the man's pocket.

'You've been very kind,' said the customer. 'Just one more thing. Where is the men's room?'

'Out the door,' said Santa, 'turn left, walk two blocks, and there's one in a filling station on the corner.'

Helping Hand!

Santa was on the road hitch hiking on a very dark night and in the middle of a storm. The night was rolling and there was no vehicle in sight.

The storm was so strong that he could hardly see a few feet ahead of him. Suddenly, he saw a car coming towards him and waved for it to stop.

Unthinkingly, Santa got into the car and closed the door only to realize that there was nobody behind the wheel! The car starts very slowly.

Santa looks at the road and sees a curve coming his way. Scared, he starts to pray, begging for his life. He hasn't come out of shock when, just before the car hits the curve, a hand appears through the window and moves the wheel. The hand appears every time they are approaching a curve.

Gathering his strength, Santa gets out of the car and runs

all the way to the nearest town. Wet and in shock, he goes into a bar, asks for two shots of whiskey, and starts telling everybody about the horrible experience he just went through.

A silence envelops the bar.

About half an hour later, two guys walked into the same bar and one said to the other, 'Look, that's the asshole who got in the car while we were pushing it!'

Bouquet of Roses

Banta was in love with a beautiful girl.

One day, she told him that her birthday was on the following day. Banta told her he would send her a bouquet of roses; one rose for each year of her life.

That evening, Banta called the local florist and ordered twenty-one roses with instructions that they be delivered first thing the next morning.

As the florist was preparing the order, he decided that since Banta was such a good customer, he would put an extra dozen roses in the bouquet.

Poor Banta, he was never able to find out what made the young girl so angry.

Too Improved

'Preeto and I are going to get a divorce,' said Banta.

Santa was stunned. 'Why? What happened? You two seem so happy together'

'Well' he said, 'ever since we got married, Preeto has tried to change me. She got me to stop drinking, smoking, running around at all hours of the night and more. She taught me how to dress well, enjoy the fine arts, gourmet cooking, classical music and how to invest in the stock market.'

'Are you a little bitter because she spent so much time trying to change you?' Santa probed.

'Nah, I'm not bitter. Now that I'm so improved, she just isn't good enough for me.'

Woman's Ears!

Banta lost both his ears in an accident. No plastic surgeon could offer him a solution till he got to know about a very good surgeon in Mumbai and went to him.

The new surgeon examined him, thought for a while, and said, 'Yes, I can put you right.'

Banta goes back to his hotel after his operation.

The morning after, in a rage he calls his surgeon and yells, 'You bastard, you gave me a woman's ears.'

'Well, an ear is an ear. It makes no difference whether it is a man's or a woman 's.'

'You're wrong. I can hear everything, but I can't understand a thing!'

Baker?

Santa and his wife, Jeeto, lived in a small house in Chandigarh. One day she asked Santa to fix a cupboard door as one of the hinges was broken.

'I am a Photographer, not a carpenter. Get a carpenter to fix the door,' said Santa.

A few days later, Jeeto asked him to fix a dripping tap.

'Do I look like a plumber? I'm a photographer, not a plumber. Get a plumber to fix the tap,' replied Santa.

A week later, Santa notices that both the tap and the door have been fixed, so he asks Jeeto who fixed it.

She replied, 'I met a handyman in town and he offered to fix the door and the tap if I either bake him a cake or have sex with him'.

Santa asked 'So what kind of cake did you bake?

Jeeto replied 'Do I look like a baker?'

Santa at KBC Again

Santa is appearing on *Kaun Banega Crorepati* with Amitabh Bachchan.

Amitabh: Santa, you're up to fifty lakh, with one lifeline,

'Phone a Friend' remaining. If you get it right, the next question is worth one crore rupees. If you get it wrong, you drop back to ₹3,20,000. Are you ready?

Santa: Yes.

Amitabh: Which of the following birds does not build its own nest? Is it

A) Robin, B) Sparrow, C) Cuckoo, or D) Thrush.

Santa: I'd like to phone a friend. I'd like to call Banta.

Banta: Hello?

Amitabh: Hello Banta ji, this is Amitabh Bachchan from KBC. I have your friend Santa here who needs your help to answer the final question. The next voice you hear will be Santa's

Santa: Banta, which of the following birds does not build its own nest?

Is it A) Robin, B) Sparrow, C) Cuckoo, or D) Thrush.

Banta: Oh geez, Santa. That's simple. It's a cuckoo.

Santa: Are you sure?

Banta: I'm sure.

Amitabh: Santa, you heard Banta. Do you keep the fifty lakhs or play for one crore?

Santa: I want to play. I'll go with C) cuckoo.

Amitabh: Is that your final answer?

Pam: Yes.

Amitabh: Confident?

Santa: Yes, I think Banta's pretty smart.

Amitabh: You said C) cuckoo... And you're right! Congratulations, you have just won ONE CRORE!

To celebrate, Santa flies Banta to Ludhiana. That night, they go out to the town. As they're sipping champagne, Santa looks at Banta and asks him, 'Tell me, how did you know that it was the cuckoo that does not build its own nest?'

'It was easy,' replies Banta. 'Everybody knows that cuckoos live in clocks.'

Santa Complains

Santa heard his son reciting his homework:

'Two plus two, the son of a bitch is four; four plus four, the son of a bitch is eight; eight plus eight, the son of a bitch...'

'Shut up!' shouted a furious Santa. 'Watch your language! You're not allowed to use swear words'.

'But, Dad,' replied the boy, 'that's what the teacher taught us, and she said to recite it out loud till we learned it.'

Next day, Santa went right into the classroom to complain.

'Oh, heavens!' said the teacher. 'That's not what I taught them. They're supposed to say, "Two plus two, the sum of which is four."'

Fainting!

'How come you're late?' asks the Manager as Santa walks in the door.

'It was awful,' Santa explains. 'I was walking down Mall road and there was this terrible accident. A man was lying in the middle of the road. He'd been thrown out of his car. His leg was broken, his skull was fractured and there was blood everywhere. Thank God I took that first-aid course and all my training came back to me in a minute.'

'What did you do?' asks the Manager.

Santa says, 'I sat down and put my head between my knees to keep myself from fainting!'

Sandwiches!

Santa and Banta went into a diner and ordered two drinks. Then they produced sandwiches from their briefcases and started to eat.

The waiter became quite concerned and marched over and told them, 'You can't eat your own sandwiches here!'

They looked at each other, shrugged their shoulders and then exchanged sandwiches.

Resemblance!

Santa accidentally bumped into a woman on the street.

'I'm so sorry,' he apologized.

'That's quite all right,' the woman replied. 'You know,' she added with a smile, 'you look just like my fifth husband.'

'Wow,' said Santa. 'How many times have you been married?'

'Four.'

Lost and Found!

Having lost his donkey, Banta got down on his knees and started thanking God.

A passerby saw him and asked, 'your donkey is missing; what are you thanking God for?'

Banta replied, 'I am thanking him for seeing to it that I was not riding the donkey at that time. Else, I would have been missing too.'

The Genius Santa!

Microsoft places an ad in all the leading news papers, looking for good software professional, would be in charge of their next operating system Windows 2000. The interviews were to be conducted by Mr Bill Gates. Microsoft receives only three applications: an American, a Japanese and an Indian. They are all invited to Microsoft headquarters in Seattle for the interview.

'I will ask you only one question and your answer should decide your fate,' says Bill Gates.

The three applicants eagerly wait for the question.

'How do we achieve Windows 2000 from Windows 98?' asks Bill Gates.

The American and Japanese candidates are puzzled and

begin pondering over the question while Santa sits smiling in his chair.

After a while, the American answers, 'Fix bugs in Windows 98 for smooth transitions.'

'Get out of here,' shouts Bill Gates.

The Japanese says, 'Make Windows 2000 more user-friendly than Windows 98'.

'Get the hell out of here,' screams Bill Gates.

Gates looks at Santa.

Santa giggles and says: 'Rename Windows 98, Windows 2000'.

Gates says 'Balle, Balle. You get the job.'

Flying Banta!

Banta went to a helicopter flight training academy to learn to fly a helicopter. The owner agreed to train him. He showed Banta how to start the engine and basic procedures, and up he went. At 1,000 feet, Banta radioed, 'I'm doing great! I love it! I'm really getting the hang of it.'

The instructor watched him climb to over 3,000 feet and then watched in horror as the helicopter began a dive and crashed nearby. He ran over and pulled Banta out from the wreck and asked, 'What happened?'

He said, 'I don't know! Everything was going fine, until I got cold and turned off that big fan.'

Height of Savings!

On leaving his office and reaching the tram stop, Banta found that the tram bound for his home had just started moving. In his anxiety, to get home fast, he ran after the tram.

Eventually, it so happened that the race between the speeding tram and Banta ended with Banta reaching home, in his bid to chase the tram.

On entering the house, Banta gleefully exclaimed to his wife that he saved two rupees chasing the home-bound tram!

Mrs Banta, however, was not amused. In fact, she was quite upset and said, 'After all you are only dumb-headed. Instead of chasing the tram, if only you had chased a taxi, you could have saved fifty rupees instead of a mere two rupees.'

Ownership Issues!

Santa and Banta bought two horses. Now, the problem was that they could not differentiate between the horses.

One day, Santa cut off his horse's left ear so that it was easy to differentiate his horse from Banta's. However, Santa's enemy sees him chopping off his horse's ear and in turn, cuts off the left ear of Banta's horse.

Santa and Banta are unable to distinguish their horses.

Thus, Santa cuts off another body part of his horse and his enemy cuts off the same part of Banta's horse.

In the end, Santa's horse had no legs left and Banta's horse was left with only one leg.

The enemy went and cut the remaining leg of Banta's

horse. So, in the morning, Santa and Banta were back to the same situation. After a lot of thinking, Santa said, 'Okay, you keep the black one and I shall keep the white.'

Wrong to Sleep

Banta is not sleeping with his wife these days because somebody had told him that it was wrong to sleep with married women.

The Mail Problem!

Santa was speaking to his psychiatrist.

Santa: I'm on the road a lot and my clients are complaining that they can never reach me.

Psychiatrist: Don't you have a phone in your car?

Santa: That's a little too expensive, so I did the next best thing. I put a mailbox in my car.

Psychiatrist: Uh … How's that working?

Santa: Actually, I haven't gotten any letters yet.

Psychiatrist: And why do you think that is?

Santa: I figured it's because when I'm driving around, my zip code keeps changing.

Jesus

An Italian, a Jew and Santa were applying for the job of a detective. The chief decided to ask each applicant just one question and base his decision on that answer.

When the Jewish man arrived for his interview, the chief asked him, 'Who killed Jesus Christ?'

'The Romans killed him,' answered the Jew without hesitation.

The chief thanked him and he left. When the Italian man arrived for his interview, the chief asked the same question.

He replied 'Jesus was killed by the Jews.'

Again, the chief thanked the man who then left. Finally, Santa arrived for his interview, he was asked the same question.

He thought for a long time, before saying, 'Could I have some time to think about it?'

The chief said, 'Okay, but get back to me tomorrow.'

When Santa arrived home, his wife asked 'How did the interview go?'.

Pat came the reply, 'Great, I got the job, and I'm already investigating a murder.'

Best Goat!

One day, Santa was talking to a salesman about his goats. As they were talking, the salesman noticed that one of the goats had a wooden leg. 'What's the deal with the goat with the wooden leg?' asked the salesman.

'Oh! That's the best goat I've got. Could just be the best goat in the whole world!' said Santa. 'Six months ago, our house caught fire in the middle of the night. That goat crawled under the fence, ran to the house, beat on our bedroom window with his horns, woke us up and saved me and my family. That's the best goat I've got, best goat I've ever had, could just be the best goat in the whole world!'

'Okay, okay!' said the salesman. 'But what's the deal with the wooden leg?'

'Well, heck' said Santa, 'A good goat like that, you can't eat him all at once!'

Height of Waiting!

Santa and Banta decide to go picnicking one day. When they reach the spot, they realize they've forgotten to take whisky.

Banta offers to go and get it if Santa promised to not to eat the chicken till he got back.

Santa waits and an entire day goes by. 'Come on, I'm hungry. He is not going to come back so let me eat the chicken anyway,' says Santa to himself.

Suddenly Banta pops up from behind a tree and says, 'If you do that, I won't go!

Santa's Wish

Santa is sitting at the end of a bar. He sees a lamp at the end of the table. He walks down to it and rubs it. Out pops a genie.

'I will give you three wishes,' says the genie.

Santa thinks awhile. Finally he says, 'I want a beer that never finishes.'

With that, the genie makes a poof sound and a beer bottle appears on the bar.

Santa starts drinking it and right before it is gone, it starts to refill.

The genie asks about his next two wishes.

'I want two more of these,' says Santa.

War Veterans

Santa mistakenly gets on a bus full of war veterans, but upon discovering it is going his way, decides to stay on.

He sits next to a guy who jerks his head to the left every few seconds.

This really bothers Santa so he asks him, 'What's wrong with you?'

'I got this in the war,' says the man.

Santa finds this pretty disturbing so he switches seats.

The second guy he sits next to has uncontrollable spastic twitches in his right leg, causing him to kick the seat in front of him.

'What is wrong with you?' asks Santa.

Again the answer is, 'I got this in the war.'

Santa moves. The third guy Santa sits next to begins flailing his left hand.

Santa says, 'Let me guess, you got that in the war?'

His reply was, 'No, I got it out of my nose. I can't get it off of my hand.'

Cuckoo Clock

Just after Santa got married, he was invited out for a night with his friends.

Santa told his wife, Jeeto, that he would be home by midnight.

The hours passed and the beer was flowing freely. At around 2.30 a.m., Santa who was drunk as a skunk headed for home.

Just as Santa was getting through the door, the cuckoo clock in the hall cuckooed three times. He realized that his wife might wake up, so he cuckooed another nine times. Santa was proud of himself for having a quick solution at hand even when smashed.

Next morning, his wife, Jeeto asked him what time he got in and he said twelve o clock.

She didn't seem disturbed at all and then told him that they needed a new cuckoo clock.

When Santa asked her why, Jeeto said, 'Well, it cuckooed three times, said "oh crap," cuckooed four more times, cleared it's throat, cuckooed another three times, giggled, cuckooed twice more and then farted.'

By Default!

At an evening party, the guests were asked to take part in a game in which everybody was to make a face and the one who made the worst face would win the prize. It seemed as if all did their best at making the worst face. The judge went up to

Banta who was sitting alone in a corner.

Judge: Sir, I think you have won the prize. Allow me to…

Banta: Excuse me, but I was not playing at all!

Talking Parrot!

Santa's wife, Jeeto, goes into a pet store one day.

She says to the clerk, 'I need a pet to keep me company.'

'Well,' replies the clerk. 'How about this nice parrot? He'll talk to you.'

'Hey, that's great.'

She buys the parrot and takes him home. Next day, Jeeto comes back to the pet store.

'You know, that parrot isn't talking to me yet,' she says.

'Hmmm, let's see,' says the clerk. 'I know! You buy this little ladder for his cage. He'll climb the ladder and then he'll talk.'

'Okay.' Off she goes with a newly purchased ladder.

Next day, Jeeto comes back to the pet store.

'Hey, that parrot still hasn't said a word,' Jeeto says to the pet store clerk.

He thinks for a minute. 'How about this little mirror?' he says. 'You hang it at the top of the ladder. The parrot will climb the ladder, look in the mirror and then he'll talk to you.'

'Okay,' says Jeeto and goes home having bought the mirror.

The next day, Jeeto is back in the shop.

'Well, I'm getting a bit discouraged,' she says. 'That parrot isn't talking to me yet.'

The clerk scratches his head. 'Let me think. Aha! Try this bell. You hang it over the mirror. The parrot will climb the ladder, look in the mirror, ring the bell, and then he will surely talk to you!'

'Well, all right, I'll give it a try,' says Jeeto. And she buys the bell and takes it home.

The next day, Jeeto comes back to the pet shop mighty distressed.

'What's wrong?' asks the clerk.

'My parrot...well, he died,' was the quiet reply.

'Oh no! I'm so sorry for your loss!' exclaimed the clerk. 'But I have to ask you, did the parrot ever say anything to you?'

'Oh yes, he said one thing, right before he died,' Jeeto replied.

'Well, what did he say?' asked the clerk.

Jeeto says, 'He said, "DOESN'T THAT STORE CARRY ANY FOOD?"'

Golden Cafe

Once Santa ends up getting drunk at a place called the Golden Cafe.

He comes home and tells his wife, Jeeto, 'You wouldn't believe it. At the Golden Café, the floor is gold, the ceiling's gold, the chandelier is gold, even the urinals are made of gold!'

Jeeto doesn't believe him and calls up the place to check for herself. 'Is it true that your floor is made of gold?' she asks the manager.

'Yes,' says the manger.

The wife continues down the list. 'Is it true that even your urinals are made of gold?'

The manager turns around to another guy and says, 'Hey, I think we found the guy who messed up your saxophone last night.'

The Eternal Cure?

Banta (morosely): My buffalo is ill. Wasn't your buffalo down with the same illness last year?

Santa: Yes

Banta: What medicine did you give your buffalo?

Santa: I gave her 250 grams of opium.

Banta goes home and gives his ailing buffalo the medicine prescribed by Santa. The two friends meet the next day and Banta tells Santa that his buffalo had died.

Banta: I am not surprised. Even my buffalo died after taking the opium.

Reading Glasses!

Banta went to an eye specialist to get his eyes tested and asked, 'Doctor, will I be able to read after wearing glasses?'

'Yes, of course,' said the doctor, 'why not.'

'Oh! How nice,' said Banta joyously. 'I have been illiterate for so long.'

The Double-decker

Santa and Banta landed up in Mumabi. They managed to get into a double-decker bus.

Santa somehow managed to get the seat below, but Banta got pushed to the top.

After a while, when the rush had reduced, Santa went upstairs to see Banta. Banta, scared to death, was clutching the seats in front with both hands.

'Banta! What the heck's going on? Why are you so scared? I was enjoying my ride down there.'

Scared, Banta replies. 'Yeah, but you have got a driver.'

Lucky Santa!

Santa goes into his son's room to wish him goodnight. His son is having a nightmare—Santa wakes him and asks his son if he is okay. His son replies he is scared because he dreamt that his aunt had died. Santa assures the son that Auntie is fine and sends him to bed.

The next day, Auntie dies. One week later, Santa again goes into his son's room to wish him goodnight. His son is having another nightmare—Santa again wakes his son. The son this time says that he had dreamt that his grandmother had died. The father assures the son that she is fine and sends him to bed.

The next day, the grandmother dies. One week later, Santa again goes into his son's room to wish him goodnight. His son is having another nightmare, he again wakes his son. The son says that he had dreamt that his daddy had died. The father

assures the son that he is okay and sends the boy to bed.

Santa goes to bed but cannot sleep because he is terrified. The next day, Santa is scared for his life- he is sure is going to die. After dressing he drives very cautiously to work fearful of a collision. He doesn't eat lunch because he is scared of food poisoning. He avoids everyone for he is sure he will somehow be killed. He jumps at every noise, starts at every movement and hides under his desk.

After the day's work, upon walking in his front door, he finds his wife, Jeeto. 'Good God, Dear,' he proclaims, 'I've just had the worst day of my entire life!'

Jeeto responds, 'You think your day was bad. This morning the milkman dropped dead on the front steps!'

Amazing Ball

A golfer, playing a round by himself, is about to tee off, when Banta, a salesman, runs up to him and yells, 'Wait! Before you tee off, I have something really amazing to show you!'

The golfer, annoyed, says, 'What is it?'

'It's a special golf ball,' says Banta. 'You can never lose it!'

'What do you mean,' scoffs the golfer, 'you can never lose it? What if you hit it into the water?'

'No problem,' says Banta. 'It floats, and it detects where the shore is and spins towards it.'

'Well, what if you hit it into the woods?'

'Easy,' says Banta. 'It emits a beeping sound and you can find it with your eyes closed.'

'Okay,' says the golfer, impressed. 'But what if your round goes late and it gets dark?'

'No problem, Sir. This golf ball glows in the dark! I'm telling you, you can never lose this golf ball!'

The golfer buys it at once.

'Just one question,' he says to Banta. 'Where did you get it?'

'I found it.'

Banta in Space!

Two dogs, Rubi and Moti, and Banta were sent to outer space.

The ground control issues commands 'Rubi!'

'Woof!'

'Press the red button.'

'Woof! Woof!'

'Moti!'

'Woof!'

'Press the white button.'

'Woof! Woof!'

'Banta!'

'Woof.'

'Stop barking, feed the dogs and don't touch anything!'

What to Wash!

Banta goes to a hotel and eats heartily. After eating he goes to wash his hands but starts washing the basin instead. The manager comes running and asks him, 'Prahji, aap kya kar rahe ho?'

Banta replies, 'Oye, tumne hi to idhar board lagaya hai, "Wash Basin."'

Santa's Prescription

Outside a pharmacy on a busy street, a poor man is clutching onto a pole for dear life. He is neither breathing, nor moving, or twitching a muscle but just standing there, frozen.

The pharmacist, seeing this strange sight in front of his shop, goes up to his assistant, Santa, and asks, 'What's the matter with that guy? Wasn't he in here earlier?'

Santa replies, 'Yes he was. He had the most terrible cough and none of my prescriptions seemed to help.'

Pharmacist says, 'He seems to be fine now.'

Santa replies, 'Sure, he does. I gave him a box of the strongest laxatives in the market. Now he won't dare cough!'

My Name is...

Santa had arrived early at the stadium for the first cricket game of the series only to realize that he had left his ticket at home. Not wanting to miss the first inning, he went to the ticket booth and stood in a long queue for another ticket. After an hour's wait, he was just a few feet away from the booth when a voice called out, 'Hey, Banta!' He looked up, stepped out of line and unsuccessfully tried to find where the voice was coming from. Then he realized he had lost his place in the queue and had to go back to the end of the line and wait all over again.

After purchasing his ticket, he went to buy a coke. The line at the refreshments stand was also very long but since the game hadn't started he decided to wait. Just as he got to the window, a voice called out 'Hey, Banta!' Again, he tried to find the voice and got out of line as he wandered looking for the source of the voice.

He was very upset as he got back in line for his coke. Finally, with his coke in hand, he took his seat eager for the game to begin when he heard the voice calling, 'Hey, Banta!'

Furious, he stood up and yelled at the top of his lungs, 'My name isn't Banta!'

Punch Me

Santa and Banta are at work, digging a hole. Banta says, 'Why is that guy sitting under the tree while we do all the work?'

Since Santa didn't have an answer, he thinks of going up to the guy and ask him instead.

The guy says, 'Because I have intelligence.'

Santa says, 'What's that?'

He stands up and says, 'Punch me as hard as you can.'

Santa winds up and punches him, but the intelligent guy moves away and Santa ends up punching the tree. His hand is now killing him.

Santa says, 'Oh, I think I know what it is now.'

He goes back down to Banta.

Banta asks, 'So why are we doing all the work?'

Santa replies, 'Because he has intelligence.'

Banta says, 'What's that.'

Santa looks around for a tree, but doesn't see one, so he puts his hand in front of his face and says, 'Punch my hand as hard as you can.'

Loving Wife!

Santa had been out for a few days due to ill health. At work Banta asked him how he was feeling?

'I'm better, thanks. You know, it was a wonderful experience.' he replied.

'Wonderful? How can the cold and fever be wonderful?' Banta asked Santa in stunned disbelief.

'Well, I learned that my wife, Jeeto, really loves me. You know that whenever the mailman came by or a delivery man headed toward the door, she ran out to meet them? I could hear her excitedly saying 'My husband is home! My husband is home!'

Spelling Error!

Banta was in the police department. One day he was present on the scene of a terrible accident that had body parts strewn everywhere. He was making his notes of where the pieces lay and comes across the dead body's head.

He writes in his notebook: 'Head on bullevard' and scratches out his spelling error.

'Head on bouelevard, and scratches out again.

'Head on boolevard...'scratch...scratch...scratch.

He looks around and sees that no one is looking at him. He kicks the head. 'Head on curb.'

Road Painters

Santa, Banta and their friend, Sunny, applied for the job of road painters. Their employer told them they would all work for three days and whoever painted the most would get the job.

At the end of the first day, Sunny had painted 4 miles, Banta had painted 3.5 miles, and Santa had painted 10 miles. The employer was happy and said the job was Santa's.

The next day, Sunny painted 6 miles, Banta painted 7 miles, and Santa 5 miles. The employer told Santa not to worry as he still had a good lead.

On the third day Sunny had painted 7 miles, Banta painted 8 miles, and Santa could only do 2 miles.

The employer was disappointed and asked Santa, 'What went wrong, you were doing so good?'

Santa said, 'Well, that bucket of paint kept getting further and further away.'

The Plane Ride!

There were three guys on a plane. The first guy ate an apple and decided to throw it out of the plane. So he threw it out just before they were to land. On landing, they saw a little girl crying. They asked her what was wrong. She said, 'I was just sitting here playing when an apple fell out of the sky and hit me on the head.'

They said, 'That sucks'

Then they took off again and the second guy threw an orange out of the plane. When they landed, there was another little girl crying. They asked her what was wrong and she said the same thing as the other girl except, that an orange hit her on the head.

They took off again and just before they landed the third guy threw a bomb off of the plane. When they landed they saw Banta laughing.

So they asked Banta, 'Why are you laughing, what's so funny?'

Banta said, 'I farted and my house blew up.'

Dirty Mind!

Santa, the biology teacher, called asked his student, Neha. 'Can you tell me which is the body part that, under the right conditions, expands to six times its normal size and state the conditions.'

Neha gasped and said in a huff, 'Why, Sir? That is an inappropriate question and my parents are going to hear of it when I get home!' She sat down, red-faced.

'Sunita, can you give me the answer?' asked Santa.

'The pupil of the eye, under dark conditions,' said Sunita.

'Correct. Now Neha, I have three things to say to you. First, you have not studied your lesson. Second, you have a dirty mind. And third, you are going to be disappointed someday!'

Silver Jubilee

Banta and Preeto decided to celebrate their 25th Wedding Anniversary with a trip to Mumbai. When they entered the hotel and booked a room, a young woman dressed in a very short skirt tried to get friendly with Banta who brushed her off.

Preeto objected. 'That young woman was nice, and you were so rude.'

'Preeto, she's a prostitute.'

'I don't believe you. That sweet young thing?'

'Let's go up to our room and I'll prove it.'

In their room, Banta called at the reception and asked for the girl to come to room 326.

'Now,' he said, 'you hide in the bathroom with the door open wide enough to be able to hear us, okay?'

Soon, there was a knock on the door. Banta opened it and girl walked in, swirling her hips provocatively.

Banta asked, 'How much do you charge?'

'Ten thousand for basic, thirty thousand for special services.'

Even Banta was taken aback. 'Ten thousand? I was thinking in the range of two thousand.' The girl laughed derisively. 'You must really be a hick if you think you can buy sex for that price.'

'Well,' said Banta, 'I guess we can't do business. Goodbye.'

After she left, Preeto came out of the bathroom. She said, 'I just can't believe it!'

Banta said, 'Let's forget it. We'll go have a drink, then eat dinner.'

At the bar, as they sipped their cocktails, the girl came behind Banta, pointed slyly at Preeto, and said, 'See what you get for two thousand rupees!'

Wedding Ring!

At the cocktail party, Mrs Santa asked Mrs Banta, 'Aren't you wearing your wedding ring on the wrong finger?'

Mrs Banta, 'Yes, I am. I married the wrong man.'

Landing Problem

Once Santa and Banta try to land an airplane in the States. They start descending and as they touch the ground Santa screams, 'the runway is ending.'

Banta swiftly gets the plane back up in the air. They make a big turn and start descending again. The moment they touch the ground, Santa screams again 'Get the plane up, the runaway is ending.'

Banta swiftly gets the plane back up in the air. They make a big turn and start descending again. This goes on for some time.

During their fourth descent Santa says, 'Look at those stupid

Americans, they build this huge and expensive airport but with such a short runaway.'

'I know,' says Banta. 'But look how wide they made it.'

On and Off!

Santa and Banta wanted to go camping. They attached the trailer to their car. Santa wanted to make sure that the car was in good condition before they start. So, he asked Banta to go in front of the car to check the headlights. Santa switched the headlights on.

'Yeah! It is working!' said Banta.

Then Santa switched on the High beam.

'Yeah! It is working!'

Santa asked Banta to go to the rear side of the car to check the brake lights. Santa slammed on the brake and Banta yelled 'Yeah! It is working!'

Santa wanted to check the left indicator and switched it on.

Then Banta started 'It is working! ooops! It is not working... It is working! ooops... It is not working!'

Hard Drive!

Santa and Banta are employed in a computer hardware store as movers. One day both of them are asked to move some computers. Santa being energetic that day does not feel the computer to be heavy at all. At the same time, he sees that Banta is struggling very hard to lift his computer.

At this Santa says, 'Why Banta, my computer has 500 MB hard disk yours has just 250, even then you cannot lift it?'

At this Banta thinks for a while and replies 'That is right, but my hard disk is full and yours is empty'

Casual Leave!

Banta's boss asked him, 'Why didn't you take leaves due to you this year?'

'Sir, I needed some rest,' replied Banta.

Bitch!

Santa is driving up a steep, narrow mountain road. A woman is driving down the same road.

As they pass each other, the woman leans out the window and yells, 'PIG!!'

Santa immediately leans out his window and replies, 'BITCH!!'

They each continue on their way and as Santa rounds the next corner, he crashes into a pig in the middle of the road.

Phone Book!

Santa stormed up to the front desk of the library and said, 'I have a complaint!'

'Yes, Sir?' said the librarian looking up at him.

'I borrowed a book last week and it was horrible!'

Puzzled by his complaint the librarian asked 'What was wrong with it?'

'It had way too many characters and there was no plot whatsoever!' said Santa.

The librarian nodded and said, 'Ahhh. So you must be the person who took our phone book.'

Mother-in-Law

Standing at the edge of the lake, a man saw a woman flailing about in the deep water. Unable to swim, the man screamed for help. Banta ran up.

The man said, 'My wife is drowning and I can't swim. Please save her. I'll give you ₹500.'

Banta dove into the water. In ten powerful strokes, he reached the woman, put his arm around her and swam back to the shore.

Depositing her at the feet of the man, Banta said, 'Okay, where's my five hundred?'

The man said, 'Look, when I saw her going down for the third time, I thought it was my wife. But this is my mother-in-law.' Banta reached into his pocket and said, 'Just my luck. How much do I owe you?'

Deer Hunt!

Santa and Banta go hunting. Santa had never gone hunting while Banta had been hunting for most of his life. When they get to the woods, Banta tells Santa to sit by a tree and not make a sound while Banta checks out a deer stand.

After Banta gets about a quarter of a mile away, he hears a blood-curdling scream. He rushes back to Santa and yells, 'I thought I told you to be quiet!'

Santa says, 'Hey, I tried. I really did. When those snakes crawled over me, I didn't make a sound. When that bear was breathing down my neck, I didn't make a peep. But when those two chipmunks (squirrels) crawled up my pants and said, 'should we take them with us or eat them here?' I couldn't keep quiet anymore!'

Evil of Drugs

Banta and one of his friends were picked up by the cops for using drugs and presented in court.

The judge said, 'You seem like nice men, and I'd like to give you a second chance rather than jail time. I want you to go out this weekend and try to show others the evils of drug use and get them to give up drugs forever. I'll see you again in court on Monday.'

Banta and his friend were in court on Monday and the judge said to the first one, 'How did you do over the weekend?'

'Well, your honour, I persuaded seventeen people to give up drugs forever.'

'Seventeen people? That's wonderful. What did you tell them?'

'I used a diagram, your honour. I drew two circles like this and told them the big circle was their brain before drugs and the small circle was their brain after drugs.'

'That's admirable,' said the judge. 'And you, how did you do?' the judge asked Banta.

Banta, 'Well, your honour, I persuaded one hundred and fifty people to give up drugs forever.'

'One-hundred-fifty people! That's amazing! How did you manage to do that?'

Banta said, 'Well, I used a similar approach. I said, "this small circle is your asshole before prison and..."'

Hurts to Touch!

Santa went to a doctor and said, 'Doctor, my whole body is aching. Everywhere I touch, it hurts.'

The doctor asked Santa to touch his elbow. Santa touched his elbow and winced in genuine pain.

The doctor was surprised and asked Santa to touch his head. Santa touched his head and jumped in agony.

The doctor asked him to touch his knee and the same thing happened.

The doctor was stumped and ordered a complete examination with X-rays and told Santa to come back after two days.

Santa came back two days later and the doctor said, 'We have found your problem.'

'Oh yes? What is it?' asked Santa.

'You have broken your finger!' replied the doctor.

Confidential Fax!

Santa: Do you know anything about this fax-machine?

Banta: A little. What's wrong?

Santa: Well, I sent a fax and the recipient called back to say all she received was a blank page. I tried it again and the same thing happened.

Banta: How did you load the sheet?

Santa: I didn't want anyone else to read it by accident, so I folded it so only the recipient would open it and read it.

Responsible?

Two weeks after Santa is transferred to a new department, his old boss got a phone call.

'You told me Santa was a responsible worker!' yelled the furious head of department.

'Oh, he is,' she confirmed. 'In the year he worked in my department, the computer went down five times and had to be completely reprogrammed, the petty cash got misplaced six times and I developed an ulcer. And each time Santa was responsible.'

Happy Birthday!

Santa walks into a bar in Ludhiana and asks for three beers. The bartender puts them up and then watches Santa go through a peculiar ritual.

'Happy Birthday, happy birthday, happy birthday.' Each time he said this, he would drink the beer. He would then pay and walk out of the bar.

One year later, he enters the same bar again and orders the same drink. The bartender watches him go through the same ritual. Curious, he asks Santa why.

'Well' Santa says, 'I have a friend in Canada and a friend in Sydney. We have our birthdays on the same day. We can't be together so we have agreed that on this day we will each go into our local pub and have a round of drinks for each other. We have been doing this for twenty years since we were eighteen.'

The next year Santa comes in and asks the bartender for two beers. The bartender, a bit taken aback, places two beers in front of Santa and watches him say 'Happy Birthday, Happy Birthday!'

The bartender asks, 'So which one died?'

'No one.'

'But you only ordered two drinks!'

'Yeah, well, I've given up drinking.'

Running Luck?

Santa and his girlfriend were driving along one day. He noticed that she kept looking at him and smiling. Then she leaned over and whispered in Santa's ear, 'Can you drive using only one hand?'

'I sure can' Santa grinned, thinking his luck was in.

'Good!' she said, 'Then wipe your nose; it's running!'

Intruder

Santa and his wife, Jeeto had just gone to bed. Just as Santa was about to fall asleep, his wife shook him and said, 'I hear someone breaking in.'

At least two nights a week, for twenty years, Santa had gone through this. He knew that the only way he would get any rest was to go and check it out. So this time too, he went out for a routine check.

When Santa entered the den, he was surprised by an intruder. The man pointed a gun at him and continued to rob the house. As the thief was about to leave, Santa said, 'You have to go and meet my wife, Jeeto.'

The thief said, 'Why on earth would you want me to meet your wife?'

Santa replied, 'Well, she's been expecting you for twenty years.'

No Risks

Santa went on a vacation to the Middle East with his family including his mother-in-law. During their vacation and while they were visiting Jerusalem, Santa's mother-in-law died.

With the death certificate in hand, Santa went to the Indian Consulate Office to make arrangements to send the body back to Punjab for a proper funeral ceremony.

The Consul, after hearing about his mother-in-law's the death, told Santa that sending the body back to India for cremation would be very expensive. It could cost as much as fifty thousand rupees. The Consul then advised Santa that in most cases the person responsible for the remains normally decides to cremate the body here. This would cost very less.

Santa thinks for some time and answers, 'I don't care how much it will cost to send the body back; that's what I want to do.'

The Consul, after hearing this, says 'You must have loved your mother-in-law very much considering the difference in price.'

'No, it's not that,' says Santa. 'You see, I know of a case many years ago of a person that was buried here in Jerusalem. On the third day he arose from the dead! I just can't take that chance.

Hit it Hard!

An old blacksmith realized he was soon going to quit working. So he picked out Santa to become his apprentice. The old fellow was crabby and exacting.

'Don't ask me a lot of questions,' he told Santa. 'Just do whatever I tell you to do.'

One day the old blacksmith took an iron out of the forge and laid it on the anvil.

'Get the hammer over there,' he said. 'When I nod my head, hit it real good and hard.'

Now the town is looking for a new blacksmith.

Saved a Lot!

Santa and Banta once go on a fishing trip. They spend a fortune in renting all the equipment—the reels, the rods, the wading suits, the rowboat, the car, and even a cabin in the woods. The first day they go fishing but they don't catch anything. The same thing happens on the second and the third day. It goes on like this until finally, on the last day of their vacation, Santa catches a fish. They are very depressed while they're driving home.

Santa turns to Banta and says, 'Do you realize that this one lousy fish we caught cost us fifteen hundred bucks?' Banta says, 'Wow! Then it's a good thing we didn't catch any more!'

Banta as a Trainee!

Banta joined a big MNC as a trainee. On his first day, he dialed the pantry and shouted into the phone, 'You Rascal! Get me a coffee quickly!'

The voice from the other side responded, 'You fool you've dialed the wrong extension! Do you know who you're talking to?'

'No', replied Banta.

'It's the Managing Director of the company, you fool!'

Banta shouted back, 'And do you know who you are talking to, you fool?'

'No', replied the Managing Director.

'Good!', replied Banta put down the phone!

Train on Platform!

Banta is standing on platform No. 1 waiting for the Punjab mail to arrive. There is an announcement 'Passengers to note. Train No. 234 Punjab mail from New Delhi will be arriving on platform No. 1 shortly.'

Hearing this, Banta panicks. He immediately picked up his baggage, jumped on to the railway track and stood there.

Banta & Lord

Banta: Lord, is it is true that to you a thousand years is like a second?

God: Yes, that's true.

Banta: And is it also true that to you, a thousand crore is like a paisa?

God: Yes, that's so.

Banta: Then, Lord, could you give me a thousand crore?

God: Yes, in a minute.

The Tramp

Banta was walking home late one night when he came upon an intoxicated tramp on the sidewalk. Wanting to help, he asked the man, 'Do you live here?'

'Yesh,' the man slowly replied.

'Would you like me to help you upstairs?' Banta asked.

'Yesh,' the man said.

When they got to the second floor, Banta asked, 'Is this your floor?'

'Yesh,' the man replied.

Banta got to thinking that maybe he didn't want to face the man's irate wife because she may think he was the one who got the man drunk. So, he opened the first door he came to and shoved him through it, then went back downstairs.

But lo and behold when he went back outside, there was another tramp lying on the sidewalk. So Banta asked that man, 'Do you live here?'

'Yesh.'

'Would you like me to help you upstairs?'

'Yesh.'

Banta took him upstairs and shoved him inside the same door with the first tramp. Then went back downstairs, where, to his surprise, there was another tramp.

Banta started over to him. But before he got to him, the tramp staggered over to a policeman and cried, 'For God's sake, offisher, protect me from thish man. He'sh been doing nothing all night long but takin' me upstairsh and throwing me down the elevator shaft!'

Total Mayhem...

Banta comes home from work to find total mayhem at home. The kids were outside still in their pyjamas playing in the mud and muck. There were empty food-boxes and wrappers all around. As he proceeded into the house, he found an even bigger mess.

Dishes on the counter, dog-food spilled on the floor, a broken glass under the table and a small pile of sand by the back door. The family room was strewn with toys and various items of clothing and a lamp had been knocked over.

Banta headed up the stairs, stepping over toys, to look for his wife, Preeto. He was beginning to worry that she may be ill, or that something had happened to her. He found her in the bedroom, still in bed with her pyjamas on, reading a book.

Preeto looked up at him, smiled and asked how his day went. Banta looked at her bewildered and asked, 'What happened here today?'

She again smiled and answered, 'You know, every day when you come home from work and ask me what I did today?'

'Yes,' Banta said.

Preeto answered, 'Well, today I didn't do it!'

What's That Noise?

Banta is looking to buy a saw to cut down some trees in his back yard. He goes to a chainsaw shop and enquires about various kinds of chainsaws. The dealer tells him, 'Look, I have a lot of models, but why don't you save yourself a lot of time and get the top-of-the-line model. This chainsaw will cut a hundred trees for you in one day.'

Banta takes the chainsaw home and begins working on the trees. After cutting for several hours and only cutting two trees, he decides to quit. He thinks there is something wrong with the chainsaw.

'How can I cut for hours and only cut two trees?' Banta asks himself. 'I will begin first thing in the morning and cut all day,' Banta tells himself.

So, the next morning Banta gets up at 4:00 a.m. and keeps cutting till nightfall but still manages to cut only five trees. Banta is convinced that the saw is bad.

'The dealer told me it would cut one hundred cords of wood in a day, no problem. I will take this saw back to the dealer.'

The next day Banta brings the saw back to the dealer and explains the problem. The dealer, baffled by Banta's claim, removes the chainsaw from the case.

The dealer says, 'Hmm, it looks fine.'

Then the dealer starts the chainsaw, to which Banta responds, 'What's that noise?'

False Alarms

An extremely modest man was in the hospital for a series of tests, the last of which had left his bodily systems extremely upset.

Upon making several false alarm trips to the bathroom, he figured that the latest episode was just that, so he stayed put.

Suddenly, however, he shat in his bed and was embarrassed beyond words. In a complete loss of composure, he jumped out of bed, gathered up the bed sheets and threw them out of the hospital window.

Banta was walking by the hospital when the sheets landed on him. Banta started yelling, cursing and swinging his arms violently, in an attempt to free himself of the sheets. He ended up with the soiled sheets in a tangled pile at his feet.

As Banta stood there, staring down at the sheets, a hospital security guard who had witnessed the entire incident, walked up to him and asked, 'What the heck is going on?'

Banta, still staring down at the sheets, replied, 'I think I just beat the shit out of a ghost.'

12-Year old Scotch!

Santa walks into a bar and rudely demands a shot of 12-year old scotch. The bartender thinks 'this guy doesn't know the difference,' so he pours a shot of 2-year old scotch.

Santa takes one sip and spits it out. He promptly hollers at the bartender: 'I said 12-year old scotch, you bozo!'

Still unimpressed, the bartender pours out 6-year old scotch. Santa takes a sip and gives the same reaction. But the bartender still doesn't believe the patron knows the difference. So he pours a shot of a 10-year old scotch.

Banta's reaction remains unchanged. Finally, the bartender is convinced. He pours a glass of 12-year-old scotch. Santa takes a sip and is most satisfied.

A drunk at the end of the bar has been watching all this. He slides a shot glass down the bar to Santa and says drunkenly:

'Hey mishter, tashte this!'

Santa obliges. He promptly spits it out.

'It tastes like piss,' Santa shoots back at the drunk.

The drunk replies: 'It ish. How old am I?'

Brief!

Santa is appearing for his University final examination. He takes his seat in the examination hall, stares at the question paper for five minutes and in a fit of inspiration, takes his shoes off and throws them out of the window. His shirt, pant, socks and watch follow suit. The invigilator, alarmed, approaches him and asks what is going on.

Santa says, 'I am only following the instructions—Answer in brief.'

2nd Act of Play !

Santa: What did you think of the second act of the play?

Banta: I did not see it. In the programme it said 'Second Act- One year,' later and I could not wait that long.

Where's the Money?

The mafia was looking for a new man to make weekly collections from all the private businesses that they were 'protecting'. Feeling the heat from the police force, they decided to use a deaf person for this job; if he were to get caught, he wouldn't be able to communicate to the police what he was doing.

In his first week, the deaf collector picks up over ₹50,00,000. He gets greedy and decides to keep the money and stashes it in a safe place. The mafia soon realizes that their collection is late and sends some of their goons after the deaf collector. The goons find the deaf collector and ask him where the money is.

The deaf collector can't communicate with them, so the mafia drags him to Santa, an interpreter.

The mafia says to Santa, 'Ask him where is the money.'

'Where's the money?'

The deaf replies, 'I don't know what you're talking about.'

Santa says, 'He says he doesn't know what you're talking about.'

The hood pulls out a .38 pistol and places it on the head of the deaf collector. 'Now ask him where's the money.'

'Where is the money?'

The deaf man says, 'The 50,00,000 is in Rose Garden, hidden in the ninth tree stump on the left from the exit gate.' Santa says to the hood, 'He says he still doesn't know what you're talking about and doesn't think you have the guts to pull the trigger'

Guruji!

The headmaster of a school was reprimanding Banta. 'It has been reported that you called your history teacher gadhaa. You are fined ₹50.'

'Sir, would I be fined if I called a gadhaa my guruji?'

'Surely not.'

'That's fine, Guruji!'

Kind Banta

Preeto arrived home after a long shopping trip and was horrified to find her husband, Banta, in bed with a young, lovely thing. Just as she was about to storm out of the house, Banta stopped her.

'Before you leave, I want you to hear how this all came about. Driving home, I saw this young girl, looking poor and tired. I offered her a ride. She was hungry, so I brought her home and fed her some of the roast you had forgotten about in the refrigerator. Her shoes were worn out so I gave her a pair of your shoes you didn't wear because they were out of style. She was cold so I gave her that new birthday sweater you never wore even once because the colour didn't suit you. Her slacks were worn out so I gave her a pair of yours that you don't fit into anymore. Then as she was about to leave the house, she paused and asked, "Is there anything else that your wife doesn't use anymore?" And so, here we are!'

Milking?

Santa is sitting in the neighbourhood bar getting soused.

Banta comes in and asks Santa, 'Hey, why are you sitting here on this beautiful day getting drunk?'

Santa: Some things you just can't explain.

Banta: What happened that is so horrible?

Santa: Well if you must know, today I was sitting by my buffalo, milking her. Just as I go the bucket about full, she took her left leg and kicked it over.

Banta: That's not so bad, what's the big deal?

Santa: Some things you just can't explain.

Banta: So then what happened?

Santa: I took her left leg and tied it to the post on the left with some rope. Then I sat down and continued to milk her. Just as I got the bucket about full, she took her right leg and kicked it over.

Banta: Again?

Santa: Some things you just can't explain.

Banta: So, what did you do then?

Santa: I took her right leg and tied it to the post on the right.

Banta: So then what did you do?

Santa: I sat back down and continued to milk her and just as I got the bucket just about full, the stupid buffalo knocks over the bucket with her tail.

Banta: Wow you must have been pretty upset!

Santa: Some things you just can't explain.

Banta: So then what did you do?

Santa: Well I didn't have any more rope, so I took off the naada of my pyajama and tied her tail to a tree's hanging branch. In that moment, my pyajama fell down and my wife, Jeeto, walked in.

Dancing Duck

A circus owner walked into a bar to see everyone crowded around a table watching a little show.

On the table was an upside-down pot and a duck tap dancing on it. The circus owner was so impressed that he offered to buy the duck from its owner, Banta.

After some wheeling and dealing they settled for ₹35,000 for the duck and the pot.

Three days later, the circus owner runs back to the bar in anger. 'Your duck is a rip-off! I put him on the pot before a whole audience and he didn't dance a single step!'

'Well,' said Banta, 'Did you remember to light a candle under the pot?'

Caring Medicos!

Santa took his elderly father to a nursing home to check it out. He sat his father down on a sofa in the main aisle way and went to talk with the administrators.

Santa's father started to tilt slowly towards the left.

A Doctor came by and said, 'Let me help you.'

The Doc piled several pillows on the left side of Santa's father so he would stay upright. Santa's father started to tilt slowly to the right. An orderly noticed and put several more pillows on his right side to keep him upright. Santa's father started to lean forward when a nurse came by and piled several pillows in front of him. About this time, Santa returned. Santa, 'Well, Dad, isn't this a nice place?'

Santa's father replied, 'I guess it's okay but they won't let me fart.'

Made in the USA
Monee, IL
07 July 2026

56550056R00094